"Why are you here?"

His jaw slackened, his ethereal eyes widening. "Because I need to know."

"Know what?" Flora breathed the words, low and long. His words were an echo of the night they'd met. When their worlds collided. Both surreal entities standing in front of each other, trapped in each other's aura—in each other's presence. A moment out of time, out of place...

And here he was again. *Out of place.* Making her feel—making her react—rather than think or follow routine.

"Are you or are you not?" he asked, his voice pulling her in, trapping her in his intense gaze and locking her inside. "Pregnant?"

Lela May Wight grew up with seven brothers and sisters. Yes, it was noisy, and she often found escape in romance books. She still does, but now she gets to write them, too! She hopes to offer readers the same escapism when the world is a little too loud. Lela May lives in the UK with her two sons and her very own hero, who never complains about her book addiction—he buys her more books! Check out what she's up to at lelamaywight.com.

Books by Lela May Wight

Harlequin Presents

His Desert Bride by Demand

Visit the Author Profile page at Harlequin.com.

Lela May Wight

—

BOUND BY A SICILIAN SECRET

PRESENTS

PRESENTS™

ISBN-13: 978-1-335-58438-0

Bound by a Sicilian Secret

Copyright © 2023 by Lela May Wight

For questions and comments about the quality of this book, please contact us at CustomerService@Harlequin.com.

Harlequin Enterprises ULC
22 Adelaide St. West, 41st Floor
Toronto, Ontario M5H 4E3, Canada
www.Harlequin.com

Printed in U.S.A.

BOUND BY A SICILIAN SECRET

This book is dedicated to my editor, Charlotte. Thank you for guiding me to find the true heart of my stories.

CHAPTER ONE

HER LIFE—HER HISTORY—had been erased.

Flora Bick stared at the document in her hands. One hundred and twenty-six pages of redacted information. Thick black line after thick black line.

She'd known the risks—the fall-out. The counsellor had prepared her before this, her first visit into the big smoke without her parents. London, a city that had always felt so far away from her life in Devon. But what she hadn't expected was the pain in her chest, nor the tightening of her gut into a clenched fist.

She hadn't expected the...*grief.*

It *was* grief, wasn't it? Something had crashed into her chest, leaving a vast crater. But it wasn't empty. It was full of lots of things she couldn't place—couldn't catch. It was a tightness, a tingle, a breathlessness.

Sitting on the edge of the bed, Flora flipped

to the first page of her adoption file with trembling fingers.

It was a chronological account of her life before the farm. Before two strangers had claimed her as their own. As their daughter. But she'd been someone else's daughter, hadn't she? It had taken a broken ankle for her to find that out. To learn that she and her parents were not biologically related.

And it hurt.

The lies.

Twenty-one years of lies!

Her instinct was to run. Run hard and run fast. But where would she go? She'd chosen this hotel. Ignored the reservation for the more budget-friendly hotel her parents had booked for her, close to the train station, and walked into this hotel with its golden doors and nodding doormen dressed in white hats and gloves, offering to carry her tatty backpack for her.

Because just for today—for tonight—she wanted to experience a world that was unlike her own. A life she might have had. Who knew?

She hadn't known.

Not until she'd opened this folder.

And she'd wanted to open it in a room like this.

The ceilings were high, with sweeping patterns leading to a chandelier of dangling diamond lights. The dark oak bed almost spanned the width of the room, with layers upon layers of the softest blankets. And when she'd climbed onto it the mattress hadn't given at her weight. It had cushioned her body in a firm but gentle hug. Caressed her skin with the softest touch. And she'd let her head fall against the mountain of pillows and stared at the view.

Her eyes shot now to the floor-to-ceiling windows. She'd pulled back the heavy blue curtains with their intricate gold leaf pattern when she'd arrived, pushed open the French doors which led to nowhere but an iron railing and the view.

The skyline of London—the big city—the home of her birth, of her beginning. The place where she'd discovered the truth about herself when she'd collected her adoption file from the local authority.

She'd had to make a special request for it not to come through the post, because if it had she might never have received it. She didn't doubt for a second that her parents would have intercepted it first.

She'd pushed harder than she'd ever pushed for anything. For her parents to loosen the reins. To trust her to collect her file unaccompanied. To be in this big city with its bright lights and buildings taller than the clouds. So she could be away from the farm, away from them, away from expectation.

She hadn't wanted the people who'd raised her to sugar-coat the impact. All her life they'd been sprinkling sugar over sour apples. Peeling off the tart skin. Removing the core. Presenting perfectly bite-sized pieces for her to consume. Just the way they'd presented life to her. In perfect chunks. Removing the bruises. Sweetening the distasteful…

It made sense now. The over-protectiveness. The never letting her fall from the straight and narrow, never allowing her to make her own choices. They'd never let her make her own choices because she was missing vital information, wasn't she?

The strong pain medication she'd required for her badly broken ankle was something that she should be careful with because of the risks. Risks that may be compounded because of her history. Because of her genes. Her possible addictive personality. Her compulsions…

Like buying the dress.

She hadn't been able to resist, had she? Not the dress—not the hotel.

She looked at her bare arms, at her shoulders encased in tight-fitting emerald-green. She'd never worn a fancy frock before. Never had the opportunity. But she'd bought this. Wanted to have it. *Needed* to have it. Whipped it off the charity shop hanger and claimed it as hers.

Because addiction ran in her blood, didn't it? Her mother's blood.

She'd never known her mother. She never would. The file was clear on one thing: her biological mother was dead. The way of life she'd chosen above her own flesh and blood had taken her to an early grave.

What else ran in Flora's blood? A sickness like her mother's? How would she ever know when her life was...*redacted*?

She stood. The file slid from her silk-clad thighs to land at her feet. The symbolism crushed her. Her life, her history, tossed to the ground as if it meant nothing. And it *was* nothing, wasn't it?

This file, these black-and-white-striped papers she'd agonised over for months, had only increased her need to know more. The need to know where and who she came from. It hadn't eased her curiosity, only raised more questions.

And more doubt.

She wasn't who she'd thought she was. She was not Flora Bick, daughter of dairy farmers. She was the abandoned child of a drug addict. Father unknown.

Placing a hand to her chest, Flora struggled to drag in a breath. She felt trapped.

She ran then.

Ran fast.

She didn't close the door behind her. She did nothing but make her feet move along the corridor with abstract art on its every wall and past windows offering a different view with every step away from her hotel room to bring her to a spiralling staircase.

Flora fingered the golden banister and hesitated. There would be people if she went down the stairs. No space to move because she'd be shoulder to shoulder with strangers stealing all the air she needed. Just the way her parents stole it at home. Giving her no room. No air. No space to think.

She wasn't in her little village any more, straddling the border between North Devon and Cornwall. There was nowhere to seek sanctuary. No windblown forest to hide in. There were no fields. No cows. No beach to comb. She was in a city. A great big city. With every corner, every street, full of people living, moving, talking. Always talking.

She craned her neck, looking up at the stairs that curved around to another invisible floor. What if she kept going up?

Her chest tight, and panting, she fisted the fabric of her dress at her waist, hiked the too-long skirt above her bare feet and climbed. Seeking another place. Solitude. Sanctuary.

Breathlessly, she reached the top floor. A dead end. With her back to the wall, she leaned against it, catching her breath.

Click.

The wall behind her had moved...

Raffaele tugged the buttons loose at his throat, but the stiffness lingered. The tightness in his jaw was becoming an ache.

Every window held a light...every street was ablaze. Even the trees lining the snaking paths far below held little fires in them.

But not the *right* kind.

Not the kind that burnt. Not the kind that raged inside him. Those flickering lights all over London could be turned on and off with a switch. He did not have a switch. His fire always burned. But he kept the oxygen levels low. Never gave it room to breathe. Contained it by will. *His* will.

He pressed a palm to the floor-to-ceiling window and took a sip of the brown spiced drink in his too-tight grip. Its wetness wasn't enough to douse the heat inside him. It roared against it—against the alcohol travelling down his throat and into his gut—challenging it to take him under. Challenging him to take another sip—

spill another measure into the tumbler. Knock it back. Find oblivion. Forget for an hour. A minute. A second. Let the rage go.

For what? Peace will never be yours again.

The voice mocked him with its truth. Because he would never know peace. He'd never known peace. But sleep…? He craved it. Its blanket of shadows. Its darkness.

But he couldn't sleep.

Every time he closed his eyes he saw his *mamma.* He could not let go because he had no right to. He wasn't allowed to forget or to sleep because he was to blame. Only him.

The inquest had delivered its verdict.

No medical negligence.

He swallowed. Hard. Tried to dislodge the lump in his throat. She'd been too thin. Too frail. She'd left everything she knew, everything that brought her comfort, to live in a facility with people who didn't know her—couldn't protect her the way he could. She'd lost the battle with her depression. Died. Because the one time she'd needed him to hold her hand and pull her back from the edge he hadn't been there.

Guilty as charged.

He'd been the one to beg her to go to the facility. L'Essenza del Caso, they'd called it. The Essence of Chance. A haven to explore one's self.

To heal in safety with twenty-four-hour therapists available to talk.

His mother hadn't wanted to talk. She'd wanted his father. Still. After thirty years of abandonment…of rejection and lies.

He scrubbed a hand over his mouth but he couldn't wipe away the bitterness lingering on his lips, his tongue.

Raffaele had known his father's death would come as a blow. He'd gone home. Dropped everything to be the first tell his mother that the Count who'd discarded her as if she was nothing—a dirty little secret he'd hidden away from the world in the middle of nowhere in the Sicilian countryside with a wad of cash and a promise of 'soon'—was dead.

'Soon' was never coming.

He thought she'd scream—break things. Cry. Then come full circle to sit mute.

He'd never imagined it would be fatal.

His fingers clenched around the glass. Pain sliced through him. Acute. Searing. He imagined for a moment taking a step back, raising his arm and letting go. *With force.* Shattering the tumbler against the window. Hearing the crack as shards of glass exploded around him to glisten in the deep red carpet at his feet.

Instead, he moved, placing the glass down on a table with noiseless precision.

Control. It was all he had. All he'd ever had. The way he reacted—responded—to the world around him. That judge had sentenced him to a lifetime of regret. He'd reacted without even a flicker of his pulse in the Italian courtroom today. But inside—

His head snapped back to the window and he saw a flash, a movement. What looked like a woman shrouded in green. He watched her pad across the stone terrace. Her eyes, almost black in the darkness, scanned the space. A heart-shaped face shrouded by dark waves that rested on bare shoulders. Her collarbone, pronounced, was taut. The hollow at the base of her throat led down to a perfect V of green silk, drawing his eye to the slope of her small breasts.

The concrete city behind her was ablaze with blues and greens. And The Thames reflected deep violet streaks in the watery depths under the Millennium bridge. She was a shadow against the enveloping city in a too-long ball gown.

Her bare toes peeped out with every step beneath the hem, which dragged along the floor and trailed behind her. Amber lights on the floor guided her with each footfall. She slowed, lingering among the green leaves spiralling from pot plants to trail upwards on trellises in vivid reds and deep blues.

She looked mythical. Out of place.

There were no parties here tonight. No Christmas celebrations. None of the D-class celebrities and influencers who came to this hotel to take pretty pictures of the vintage decor, its iconic status amongst the elite lost.

That would change, in time, when his team gutted it. Put his stamp on it. His brand. *His name.* Not the Nobiltà Italiana name his father had denied him. But *his* name. *Russo.* Then the glitz and glamour of the rich who wore their ball gowns to breakfast would be a daily occurrence, but the previous owner had let standards slip. Everything except the rooms he stood in and the garden terrace outside.

Tonight, he understood the appeal.

This part of the hotel was completely shut off. The previous owner had created a secret world of opulence. A place to hide with every comfort at his disposal. Secret stairs, secret doors, secret passages behind the walls for secret access so staff could enter and leave unseen.

But *she* was not staff. He knew that because he could see her. *Clearly.*

He moved back, his thigh knocking the table, tilting the glass he'd saved from a violent end. He steadied it again by instinct, because he couldn't drag his eyes away from her. This tiny figure invading his privacy.

Raffaele lifted his hand to flick on the flood-lights and then hesitated.

She couldn't see him. Outside, where she stood, she would see nothing but a wall. A darkness. Cleverly designed glass let those inside look out, but those beyond wouldn't be aware of their existence.

His existence.

But the shadows would disappear in the light.

She'd turned her back to him, was stalking to the iron and brick balcony. Her spine was prominent, and it called to him. The need to trail his fingers along it was instant. To tilt his head. Kiss—

Kiss?

She was a trespasser.

A trespasser on his grief.

And trespassers needed to be caught.

Her hair was caught in a wild gust of wind. It danced around her shoulders. She raised her arms high and wide beside her, lifting her face to the night sky and leaning over the edge.

He forgot to breathe.

Was this a test?

Was she a messenger, sent to remind him how completely he'd failed his mother? His mother had chosen a roof. His mother had leapt to her fate.

His palm met a square silver panel on the wall. The glass shifted soundlessly to create a door.

She remained still. Standing on the edge. Protected only from falling by a waist-high iron-wrapped wall. Her arms were still outstretched, her face tilted as if she were an offering to the city. To the gods…

An offering for you? For redemption?

Raffaele moved towards her, prompted by the tug of his gut. He couldn't see her face. An inappropriate urge stormed through him to see her eyes, to look into them, to be close enough to do that.

He caught her wrist. She turned.

His breath hitched. Big brown eyes met his. His pulse slowed. He searched her gaze, watching the golden flecks in her left eye burn with something primal. Something achingly close to recognition.

But he didn't know her.

He would remember those eyes…

The delicate warmth from her body hit him. It was a caress against his prickling skin. An awareness of her femininity. The male in him responded without his permission. A low heat gathered in his gut, arrowing down to his groin. Mocking him with the ease with which his body was reacting to a familiarity that didn't belong to him.

But the air between them pulsed…throbbed.

He dragged his gaze from hers. Moved it down to where his fingers encased her small wrist. It was her pulse. That throb. It pounded beneath his thumb. And the urge to swipe his thumb against it was so clear, so overwhelming, it consumed him.

So he did it, before he could tell himself not to. He stroked against her skin. Soft. Warm. *Delicate.* But her pulse wasn't. It pounded. Fierce. Strong.

His eyes shot back to her face. The lights of London's skyline flickered around her head like a halo.

'Are you real?'

It was the most delicate of whispers. It tingled across his skin, snapping him out of the haze that had fallen over him since the inquest. Clearing the fog that had travelled with him since his *mamma's* death and plunging him straight into the depths of her eyes.

'Of course I am.' He straightened, wanting to drop her wrist but unable to will his fingers to release her. 'Are you?' she asked.

She blinked up at him, lashes fluttering rapidly. He wanted to count them. Wanted to know exactly how many dark strands it took to create such appealing shadows on her high cheekbones…

He did not ever notice a woman's eyelashes.

He stilled. His jaw hardened.

He was not himself.

'Am I asleep?' he asked, cursing his lack of control over his tongue. This moment was too surreal. Too…*something*…

'Only if I am too,' she said, bringing his attention to a bottom lip so sinful, so plump, his urge was to take it between his teeth and test its fullness.

What was wrong with him?

'And are you?' he asked.

He was hoping. But he didn't know what for. He hadn't slept for weeks. A sleep-deprived mind could conjure many things.

A vision.

A mirage of creamy flesh laced in green silk.

A woman with a too-wide mouth. Too delicate. Too soft. Too kissable.

'No,' she replied, with a gentle shake of her head. 'I'm awake.'

Reality tugged at the periphery of his mind and he released her wrist. 'Are you lost?'

'No…' Her eyes moved down his torso to his leather-tipped toes. Brown strands of silk teased forward to caress her cheeks. He clenched his fist, pushing down the urge to push her hair behind her ear. To touch her…*intimately.*

'Who showed you how to get in here?'

'No one.' She craned her neck. Her stare was like a physical caress against his too-hot skin. 'I found it by accident. I just ran…'

'Ran from where?' he asked, his gaze sweeping down over her slight frame. The dress was too big, and she was too small. 'Do you usually take an evening run in a ball gown?'

'No.'

Her lips lifted into something secretive. *Seductive.*

'I wanted to be alone. London is so busy. Noisy. Everyone's always moving. Always talking.' Her eyes held steady to his. 'But I'm done with running tonight.'

Wasn't that exactly the reason he was here, too? Why he hadn't gone back to the house he'd grown up in. Back to Sicily. He'd run from that Italian courtroom because his head had been too loud with unwanted memories. Too noisy with his own despair. And only now had his mind come to a stop, cushioned by the wide wonder of her brown eyes…

'How did *you* get up here?' she asked.

He wanted to touch the deep lines between her brows. Smooth them.

'I knew the way.'

'You did?'

'I did,' he confirmed.

'And you chose to come here?' Her eyes narrowed. 'Why?'

A rush of words bulged in his throat. Refusing to let him lie or deny this moment of grief. Deny his mother.

'To grieve.'

A smile, small and gentle, moved her lips. 'Me too.'

'And who do you grieve for?' he asked.

Because he truly wanted to know. Curiosity pushed against his consciousness, demanding to understand why on this night the fates had seen fit to throw his grief against hers. To slam their worlds together.

Her slender shoulders dipped. 'Myself...'

He frowned. 'For yourself?'

'Yes,' she said, making small continuous dips of her head.

Her answer pressed against something inside him. Something buried deep.

'Why?' he asked.

'Because—'

She sucked in a breath and he watched. Mesmerised. He itched to find the hardened peaks of her breasts pushing against the fabric of her dress. His hands would bury them—they were so small. He would be able to encase them fully in his palms...

Stop.

He rolled his shoulders. The leather jacket was too heavy on his skin. Too tight.

'Why do you grieve for yourself?' he forced himself to ask. Because she was not here for him to bury his grief inside her body. She was here for herself, to find a moment, some quietness, in a city that never slept. To find a place away from the noise. As he was.

'Because tonight,' she replied, 'I realised that the woman I was raised to be is someone else's idea of who I should have become.'

'What does that mean?'

'The woman I might have been wasn't ever given a chance to live.'

'How can you grieve for someone who never lived?'

'I'm allowing myself to grieve for all the things I wasn't allowed to have. I'm grieving for the woman I could have become. For the life I could have had. They denied it to her. *Me.* Withheld information...'

'Who are *"they"*?'

'They're not important. Not tonight.'

She blinked, shutting him out with those obscenely long lashes before piercing him with a penetrating look.

'Who are you grieving for?'

'My mother.'

Her eyes flickered over his face. Each flicker touched him. It was warm. Unnerving. Because it came from the softness inside her. A softness just for him. His abdomen tightened.

She stepped down into his space. Moved into his heat. The fire inside him spat embers into the cool winter night's air and the air between them crackled with it.

'I'm so sorry for your loss,' she said.

And he pushed down the urge to draw her closer. To embrace her grief with his own and offer her the same tenderness shining from the depth of her eyes.

He checked himself.

He did not deserve tenderness.

He was not tender.

He didn't know how to be.

'Tell me of the woman who could have lived,' he said, instead of responding to her sincerity. Because he didn't know how to.

'No,' she refused.

'Why do you not want to tell me?' he asked, his lungs tight, his words hoarse. He wanted to understand it. This idea of grieving for something that had never existed. The idea was raw, because he'd never let himself grieve for the life *he* could have had.

But did he want to grieve for the life he could have had with his father? A liar? A cheat? Because even if his father had claimed him who would have provided for his mother? Protected her?

She'd needed love too.

His guilt was loud tonight.

He shut it down. Because what did he know of love?

Nothing.

He knew only how to brush his mother's hair. Feed her.

He'd never been taught to love, and he didn't want to learn. Because love was a myth whispered in the act of seduction. *A lie.* His father had seduced his mother—a naïve girl from old Sicilia, who'd left the orphanage behind her and was seeking adventure in Roma, where she'd become a nanny to his three children.

Raffaele's half-brothers and sister.

His father had got his mother pregnant, and before his world could come tumbling down he'd hidden her away. Forgotten her and the dirty little secret that would've brought his world crashing around his knees had it been exposed. He'd fobbed her off with words like *soon* and *when the baby is grown.* He'd shut her away, out of sight, and forgotten about her.

Love was a lie.

'I don't need to tell you about her,' said the woman in green, slicing through the rage always ready beneath the surface to explode.

'Why not?'

'Because she's here…standing in front of you,' she said, pulling him out of his head and back into her eyes. 'Do you want to tell me about your mother?' she asked, and her words were…*inviting.*

'No.'

He didn't. He wouldn't deny his grief, but share his memories…? Never.

'I don't want to talk at all,' he finished, his heart thudding too loudly. His throat too dry.

'Neither do I.'

A gust of wind picked up the ends of her hair and threw them into her eyes. He wanted to strip off his jacket and lay it around her shoulders. Warm her.

'Are you cold?' he asked, before he could stop himself. 'Do you want me to protect you from the wind?'

Her lips parted. 'How…?'

A sluggish warmth spilled through his every vein, lodging a heavy heat in his gut. 'With my body.'

She moved into him, so close he could feel the whisper of her body against his. She placed her hand on his chest.

'Like this?'

'Do you think it is safe to play with strangers in the dark?' he asked, his tone laced with amusement and his words accusing. Because he did not like what was happening. This woman's touch was spiralling him into a moment where he couldn't control his responses.

'I'm not playing,' she said.

'What *are* you doing?'

'Choosing.'

'Choosing what?'

'To be present.'

'Present?' he repeated.

'To be present in this moment.'

He felt lightheaded. Suspended in time—in this moment. Locked into the essence of another human being. He could hear every rasp of her breath. Feel the thud of her heart as her chest rose and fell.

He was present in a way he never had been before.

'Who *are* you?' he demanded.

Her lips curved. Not up. Not down. But it was a movement. 'I'm not sure I can answer that.'

Her name didn't matter, he told himself. Hotel security could take her. Rid him of his little interloper. And then he could tighten the leash on whatever this reaction was he was having to her. Remember who he was. Who he'd made himself into.

But he yearned for it.

For her name.

'You don't know your name?' he asked, despite himself.

'I know the name I've been called by all my life. But I don't know if that name—the person who was given that name—is the person who's here in this moment. If it's the person I want to be any more.'

'You can refuse to tell me your name…but you will still be *you*.'

The words spilt from his lips in quick succession. He wasn't sure who he was tonight. But he knew with an unwavering certainty that he was not the man who'd flown by private jet from a courthouse in Italy to arrive in a wet and grey London.

And he wasn't the boy rattling around in a house in desperate need of repair with a woman who cared about nothing but seeing the man she loved again. He was a grown man now, and his house was always in perfect order.

'My name isn't important,' she said, slicing through his grief, his regret. 'It's only a name, isn't it? It doesn't make me *me.*'

'Doesn't it?'

'I don't want it to,' she said.

'Why?' he asked. 'A name can be everything.'

His name was everything—because he'd made it so.

'The woman I was before I came up here... the woman with her name—*my* name—is attached to people's assumptions,' she continued, her words coming at him fast and breathless. 'I want to leave all those downstairs.'

'Then who does that leave up here?' he asked. 'With me?'

'Only who I am right now,' she replied. 'A girl who doesn't want to go home,' she confessed. Uncoerced. Unprompted.

The words sitting on her lips were echoed in the flush tingeing her cheeks.

She wanted him.

'Where do you want to go, *piccolina*?'

'Do you have a room here?' she asked.

And then it roared through him. *Understanding*. Understanding of his temptation to smash the glass against the window.

Inhaling deeply, she added, 'I have a room...'

He watched the tendons in her throat constrict. Elongate.

'Would you like to go back to it?' he asked.

She shook her head, and then nodded. He saw the heat rising from her chest to tease at her cheeks.

'Yes. If it's with you.'

A desire to erase all distance between them ripped through him. To press her chest against his. *Without clothes*. To feel the tight peaks of her nipples against him.

'I am a stranger to you,' he said—because he was. But he was strange to himself tonight. Exposed. Raw.

'There's freedom in anonymity, and tonight I want to be free.'

'Free from what?' he asked.

He'd never been free to act on impulse. To follow his desires. His job was to provide. Protect.

'For once—just once—I want to *do* and not think,' she explained huskily. 'Not be told I shouldn't...not to be warned of the consequences. Not to be told how foolish I am for wanting something.'

'And what *do* you want?'

'I want you.'

She placed the palm of her hand on his cheek. Flames erupted inside him.

Her fingertips flexed against his skin. 'I'm going to kiss you now.'

Her eyes searched his, hesitantly at first, then boldly, as she recognised his desire, demanded his surrender. She was challenging him to concede. To give it up. His control.

A primal surge of lust pushed against the rage inside him. Coating the anger with something else. Something distinct that he couldn't name. He fought the urge to pull her into him. Into his warmth. He needed her consent—her permission—to lose control.

In his mind, he allowed himself to raise that glass in his too-tight grip. He readied himself to release the tumbler into the night. Because on her cue—if she gave it—he knew the glass would shatter.

'And do you want me to kiss you back?' he asked.

CHAPTER TWO

'YES,' FLORA CONFIRMED.

She swallowed down the urge to tell him she'd never been kissed, never been touched. Because did it matter? She didn't want it to. Not to her—not to him. Tonight she wanted nothing else to matter but this. Their connection.

A shiver raked through her.

Black brows arched above eyes so bright that it was as if the entire world had crawled inside them and reflected the earth's surface back from space.

'You're cold,' he said, shrugging off his jacket.

He leaned into her, bringing his arms around her back to trail the leather over her shoulders. She clung on to the lapels, pulling the jacket tightly around her. The smell of leather and the heat from his body rose to the cold tip of her nose and infiltrated her lungs.

Her stomach flipped as she found her courage to voice her confession. 'I've never—'

'Never what?'

'Kissed anyone,' she said, expecting to feel vulnerable. Embarrassed. But she didn't. She felt empowered. *Excited.*

She should be horrified. This wasn't how she'd been raised to respond to her feelings. Her wants. But she'd never felt as delicate or as strong as she did now, in her desire for this beautiful stranger.

And he was beautiful.

Her heart stuttered as she took in his broad shoulders, sheathed in a black shirt. He'd flicked the collar up, bringing her attention to the open buttons at his thick bronze neck...the fine black hairs leading down to his chest. A chest she wanted to see. She wanted to pop open those remaining buttons and run her hands over it.

Her eyes lowered to the belt encircling his lean hips, locked in place by a wide silver buckle. Dark tailored trousers clung to the hard muscle of his thighs. The fabric moulded to his muscular calves.

'Would you like me to kiss *you* first?' he asked, and her eyes flicked back to his face.

Her mouth parted. The air tasted of gunpowder and bonfires. The scent of the upcoming season.

She had been acting on impulse before, and she suddenly felt nervous. But still the need to touch and be touched destroyed any doubt that *this* was the way to behave. Even if it was not the way she'd been taught to behave.

'Yes.' Her eyes moved back to his mouth. 'I want you to kiss me first.'

Her core tightened. Deep down inside her. She knew she might never find a connection like this again. A raw, unguarded reaction. A sexual reaction.

'I want you to be my first.'

The blackness swept through the brilliance of his irises to a create a burning edge. Intense rings of smouldering energy. Blue…? Green…? Ethereal.

'Then we will start with your mouth.'

She teased her tongue over her bottom lip. 'Where else would we start?'

'There are many ways to kiss, *piccolina*. Would you like me to show you?'

'Yes,' she said. Because tonight she would say yes to all the things she knew she shouldn't.

She closed her eyes. Anticipation thrummed through her. Quickened her pulse. Her breathing. Every nerve-ending was shredded. Exposed.

She should feel ridiculous, standing here in a charity shop ball gown. But she didn't. She felt… *seen*. Wanted in a way she'd never been wanted. *For herself.* For the woman she was daring to be here, on top of the concrete jungle of London, in this secret oasis of lush green, of such opulence she could almost taste it.

Taste him.

His hands slid to the back of her neck, drawing her in closer. She didn't open her eyes. She just let herself *feel*. The pressure of his thumbs on her face. His palms warm against her throat. The heat of his chest against hers. The whisper of his breath against her lips. Sweet. Spiced.

Thunder roared through her, loud and alive, as he captured her mouth with his. His lips were silk against hers. Soft, but firm. Gentle, yet demanding. She opened for him. Let his tongue inside.

A sound burst from her lips. A gasp—a moan. He swiped his tongue inside her mouth as if to taste it. She copied him. Teasing her tongue against his. And the moan she tasted in her mouth this time was his. A guttural noise from deep in his chest.

It tasted…*powerful*.

She kissed him harder. Mimicking him. Pressing her lips to his. She slid her tongue into his mouth. Her hips instinctively pushed against him. She felt him harden.

He tore his mouth from hers and dipped his head to the underside of her ear and whispered, 'Has someone kissed you here?'

His breath tickled at her skin, bringing it to

life beneath his words. 'No,' she said huskily. A low heat dragged through her stomach, and it was getting heavier as he lingered on her throat.

His tongue flicked against her skin. 'Would you like to be?'

'Yes, please.'

His hands moved to cup her cheeks, holding her steady as he moved into the crook of her neck, millimetre by millimetre, and blew.

Warm, cold, electrified, she gasped, 'Oh...'

He sucked her skin into his mouth. Harder. Deeper. Her breathing sped up, her heart thumped, but the need for more was overwhelming. The pangs in her stomach told her there was more, and she needed to demand it.

Her hands bit into his shoulders. 'Please...' she murmured.

He dragged his kiss down the length of her throat. 'More?'

'Please!' she begged, and she didn't care. She'd worry about it later. Tomorrow.

His hands moved over her body, finding her breasts. He palmed them, cupping their heaviness, and swiped over her tender nipples.

Flora pressed her thighs together to stem the ache. The chaotic need to find release. 'More,' she breathed. *'More!'*

And he didn't deny her. He pulled down the top of her dress, exposing her breasts to the cool night's air, and his head descended. The heat of his mouth was on her, taking her nipple into his mouth—

'Oh, my God!' she cried out, her body pulsing, throbbing, as he sucked harder. Deeper.

He flicked his tongue over her nipple and the ache between her legs intensified. Muted everything but what he was doing to her body. He stopped kissing her breast, moved his mouth slowly over her chest and back up her throat, recaptured her lips. Roughly. *Urgently.*

He slipped his hand inside the slit of her dress that started just below her hipbone and feathered his fingertips along her inner thigh. A moan erupted in her throat. He pulled his hand from between her thighs to grip her hips. He cradled them in the arch of his and walked her backwards. Step by step. Until her back met a wall.

Her bare breasts pushed against the smooth fabric of his shirt, and she rubbed them against him. She felt feral. *Wild.*

He tore his mouth from hers. His breathing as ragged as her own, he said, 'Not here.'

Her fingers clenched around his muscular upper arms. 'But—' Her grip loosened, and she swallowed down the words in her mouth, because the desire to strip naked beneath the stars and push her body against his felt too wanton to say out loud.

'But what?' he pushed, his voice a hoarse rasp.

She looked at him. At the man who'd offered her nothing but gentleness even in his rampant seduction of her senses. The man who was staring at her as if she was the only living thing to exist in the universe. Sharing this moment with a stranger was the closest she'd ever been to really being herself. To reacting honestly. And she didn't want to stop being honest.

'I don't want to stop kissing,' she said, because the vast crater in her chest wasn't for the mother she wouldn't know, but for the parts of herself she'd never been given the opportunity to explore. Her motivations. Her *sexuality*. 'I don't want you to stop kissing *me*,' she corrected.

'Then I won't stop.'

A slow smile spread across his lips and she wanted to know what it felt like to *feel* his smile. But she was frozen. Entranced by the man who'd kissed her body with the city lights at his back, in the middle of a garden so beautiful it almost didn't seem real.

This didn't feel real.

She nodded because she didn't have the right words—*any* words—because all that was inside her mouth was a gasp as he dipped his head. He placed hard kisses on her throat. Between her breasts. On her stomach. And then he was on his knees, spreading the slit in her dress to reveal her white cotton panties.

He didn't look up, but kept his gaze there. Gently, he stroked at the waistband. The heart of her pulsed and clenched tight.

She gripped his shoulders and said the only thing she could. 'Please…'

His mouth sealed to the part of her that ached for him the most. The intensity was so close to the sweetest pain that she couldn't do anything but let her mouth fall open and try to breathe.

'Ahh…' She arched her neck. Her back pressed against the hard wall. She closed her eyes and gripped on to the lapels of his jacket.

A firm finger followed the seam of her panties and pulled them across. Exposing the pulsing heart of her. He licked her without the barrier of her panties. Tongued her with masterful stokes along the folds of her opening.

He pushed his tongue inside her.

Everything she'd thought she knew about her body—about the pleasure to be found with the exploration of her fingers—was obliterated, smashed to dust, as he put the pad of his thumb to her core and pulled his tongue out only to thrust it into her again.

She gasped with pleasure, loudly and fiercely.

He was unrelenting in his ministrations as he moved faster, the pace of his tongue increasing.

And she let him guide her. Guide her to a place she hadn't known existed. A place where her mind was blank all but for the driving need to be *here*. To feel the building tension in her body, getting tighter and tighter with seemingly no end. And she didn't want it to end. Didn't know how it could end without her shattering into a million pieces.

His mouth suddenly claimed her nub. His thumb moved to her opening…parting her. He slipped a finger inside her.

It was then that Flora's world exploded.

He held her steady against his mouth. Let her body rock against his lips as she screamed in ecstasy into the night sky until she had nothing left to give.

He pulled his mouth from her, easing his grip on her hips. His fingers quick, but gentle, he slid her panties back into place and shifted her dress.

He looked up. Her pulse hammered. *Hard.* Because his eyes echoed what she already knew. This shared intensity under the stars was only the beginning.

He stood, covered her bare breasts. And she let him encase her trembling body in the scent of him. The heat of him. Her throat dry, she swept her eyes over him. This man she'd let touch her body. Claim her mouth in her first kiss. *All her kisses.* She didn't want to wait. Go back to her room. She needed him. *Now.*

'Take me here,' she pleaded. 'Take me now.'

She spread her fingers, moving them over the solid arc of his shoulders, and tried to pull his mouth back to hers. But he dodged her lips and claimed the sensitive spot behind her ear.

'I have a place,' he said, and with a slide of his hand the blackness of the wall behind her turned translucent. Lights shone where none had been before. Like her dad's glasses on a sunny day…

'They're windows?' she said huskily, her eyes widening. 'Glass?'

'Yes,' he said.

'Is that how you saw me?' she asked, as what lay beyond the glass was exposed, watching as the big city revealed it hid more secrets than just the circumstances of her birth.

It hid magic in plain sight.

It was a room. Rooms.

His eyes flashed. 'Do you want to come inside?'

'Yes,' she confirmed, not recognising the huskiness of her voice.

Her stomach tightened. A tight sensation was arrowing between her legs. Making her hotter. Wetter. Her world had caught fire and it was burning around her. Everything she'd known, loved, was in question or gone. She wasn't grieving for the mother she'd never known, and she wasn't grieving for the life she'd had before she'd found out she was adopted. Because she'd been happy. She knew this in her heart. She was grieving for all the moments she might have had if she'd stood up for her own decisions, stood against her parents' fears.

They had moulded her for twenty-one years into the daughter they wanted. *Their miracle baby.* Not allowed to make mistakes, big or small. Not allowed to be anything other than the daughter they wanted.

But what did *she* want?

She wanted this.

She wanted *him*.

Flora stepped over the threshold.

'What is this place?'

It was nothing like the room she had downstairs. These rooms were...*more.* Rich... Vibrant...

'A room for the night,' he answered, his voice a seductive, deep drawl behind her.

'It's beautiful.'

A spacious entry hall with a sparkling speckled marbled floor led to a carpeted lounge scattered with rugs of silk. Heavy-cushioned sofas and high-backed chairs surrounded intimate statues of women of old, cut from black stone, and tall lamps and glided mirrors highlighted the way to more rooms.

'Magical…' she breathed.

For tonight, she belonged here. No alarm for the morning milking. No routines to maintain. Tonight she wasn't a farm hand. She wasn't the abandoned daughter of an addict. She was anonymous. Free to explore the unexplored. To explore the woman never given a voice. Never allowed to use words without trying them out in her head first.

She turned to him. Her confidence roaring, she asked, 'Is there a bedroom here?'

He nodded. His features were drawn. Tight. 'A big bedroom.'

'Will you take me to it?' she asked, praying her confidence wouldn't desert her.

When she went home—back to the farm, to her name—she wanted this night to be hers. Not her parents'. Not a fabricated experience they'd built for her. Something she'd created and experienced all on her own.

'I can…' he told her, and her heart soared. 'But only if you want it. You can leave.' He nodded towards the concealed door she'd entered by on the far side of the terrace. 'Or you can take my hand.'

He turned his hand palm forward and held it out to her like an offering.

Choice.

Wasn't that what she'd always wanted? And he'd chosen her, hadn't he? The woman she was right here and now. And she wanted to commit to whatever was happening between them. This shared moment of grief turned to passion.

She slid her fingers through his.

His hold was soft, but strong. He guided her down a long hallway towards a door and pushed open the heavy oak to reveal a room of splendour. And a four-poster bed so big it monopolised *everything...*

Tonight, she'd have no regrets. Tomorrow, she'd go home and remember the doubts—the pain.

Just once, she was going to let her herself act on feelings...

Her grip tightened on his and Flora led the way.

Towards the bed.

It took every shred of control he had left to keep his hold on her hand loose. Not to hurry. To lose himself in her gentle confidence.

Gracefully, she kept on walking towards the bed. His jacket drowned her. Cloaked her in what was his. Protected her from the heat of his gaze on her back. Hid the dip in her spine his fingers had smoothed over as he'd dragged her hips over his mouth.

She'd become his responsibility, hadn't she? It was his responsibility to protect her, to be gentle, to make her first time the best it could be.

He shouldn't be her first.

He was not gentle.

He planted his feet, stopping her from reaching the bed. *'Piccolina...'*

She turned to him. The warning died in his mouth as she released his hand, took a step backwards, and pushed his jacket from her shoulders.

It thumped to the floor. He did not look. Didn't care. Her eyes held his—trapping him, imploring him to forget everything but the desire flaring her pupils into dark discs of desire. Making them glitter. Shine just for him.

He waited.

She reached for the straps hugging the tops of her arms and pushed them down to her wrists, baring her breasts. Her fingers pushed the dress past her waist, her hips, to slide down the creamy whiteness of her thighs and land at her feet with his jacket. Then her panties. She toyed with the waistband and then, in one decisive movement, slid them to her ankles.

Stepping out of the puddle of fabric at her feet, she moved, her gaze never leaving his. The back of her legs met the mattress. The bed. She sat down. Inched her bottom up over the bedspread.

He couldn't breathe…couldn't catch his breath as she presented herself to him…let her knees fall apart. The dark triangle between her legs glistened where his mouth had been. Where he'd tasted her. Torn her apart with his mouth.

'Make love to me.'

The glass shattered.

He gripped his shirt and tore it open, the buttons popping soundlessly to the thick carpet beneath his feet. He pulled it off, along with his trousers and his boxers, kicked them all aside.

'Say it again,' he demanded, ignoring the voice in his head ordering him to tell her it was not love. She did not know what love was. Love burnt. Love hurt. And he would not hurt her. He was going to worship every inch of the body she offered to him.

Her breasts heaved. Her nipples grew taut. Tight. Almost asking for his mouth on them… his tongue. But he waited. Waited for her cue.

Her brown eyes burned black. Wide. Intense.

She was a goddess.

Her neck arched to reveal the slenderness of her throat. Her brown hair trailed back to feather the pillows he wanted to push her into. He wanted to find her mouth and take her. Possess her.

Her fingers pinched at the white bedspread. Grasped it and pulled it. 'Make love to me,' she said again.

And he wanted to be between her legs, desperately, but his last remaining strand of lucidity stopped him from moving.

Protection.

He knelt and retrieved his wallet from his jacket pocket. He pulled out a foil packet and threw the wallet to join their discarded clothes.

He stood tall. Erect. *Present.*

Her eyes fluttered to the thick length of him.

'You're…'

He was.

He held her gaze as he rolled the latex down the length of himself.

'I won't hurt you,' he promised, before he could stop himself. He didn't make promises. But she was ready, and he had no control left. Not over his mouth. Nor his body.

None.

He moved between her legs, gripped her thigh to place her calf on his lower back. Her fingers, delicate, feathered his tight jaw. He stared into her eyes because he couldn't look away. He placed the heat of himself at her entrance.

'Now…' she breathed. 'Love me *now.*'

In one thrust, he was inside her. Had pushed past the barrier that had given little resistance.

He stilled. Every muscle in his body was straining—demanding he pull out and then thrust into her again, find his release.

Her grip on his jaw tightened, refusing to let him look away.

'I'm okay,' she said huskily. 'It doesn't hurt. And I need you to move. I need you to—'

He moved. Slowly. Building his thrusts in tempo…in speed. Still, she did not look away. And he couldn't. Mesmerised by her wide eyes. Her gasping mouth. Her innocent awe. And she matched him thrust for thrust, arching her hips to take him deeper.

'Harder!' she gasped, panting her need into existence.

He gripped her hips. Thrust. Hard. *Harder.*

A deep blush bloomed on her neck…her cheeks. He could feel the heat radiating from her. The hotness filled the air between them with humidity, trapping them both inside it. In a bubble of desire.

'I… I…' she murmured between pants for air, whispering across his mouth.

It was a primitive call for release. He felt it too. The pressure.

'Oh. Oh. *Oh!*' she repeated, with every thrust of his body into hers.

He drove into her faster. *Wildly.* Until the pressure had nowhere to go but inside her.

With one last thrust the pressure inside him broke free and he lost himself to her joy, her pure amazement, and to her sighs of satisfaction mingled with his own.

'Thank you for being my first,' she said, and his hands curled possessively over her hips.

The urge to push into her again, to drive out any thoughts of *firsts*, hardened him inside her. Because with firsts came lasts, and— And *what*? He would not be her first and last kiss.

'I didn't know,' she continued, and he stilled. 'That it could be like that…so *instinctual*.'

'Instinctual?' he echoed, but he knew what this virgin didn't. Instinct did not lead to sex. You had to learn your lover.

'My body knew what it wanted and—' She shook her head, a shy smile creasing her flushed cheeks.

'Nothing else mattered?' he finished for her. Because it hadn't. Not for him. Nothing else but her.

'Exactly,' she whispered, and pressed into him, raising her chin and offering her mouth.

He let their lips meet. Closed his eyes and tasted her.

Her misguided gratitude…it was too much.

He was not nameless. He did not strip his clothes off like an adolescent teen. He didn't make love—and he certainly did not make love to virgins. He had sex. That was all this was.

He dragged his mouth from hers. Pulled himself free from her body and was on his feet, walking away from her. He needed a minute. Just a moment…

He closed the bathroom door and let himself pant. Hard. He shut his eyes and leaned back against the coldness of the door. Let it cool him until he could think, until the heat and the scent of her on his skin was not so strong. So all-consuming.

He opened his eyes and looked down.

What had he done?

The condom was torn.

Every vein bulged. Every muscle in his body turned tight. And his brain screamed that history was repeating itself. An innocent. A seduction. A baby.

Before he could stop them, memories that weren't his flashed in his head. The story he'd been told a thousand times. A girl looking for adventure, who'd found love in a place she shouldn't have.

She was exactly like his mother, before she'd had a forbidden love ripped away from her because of the conception of a baby. A child born to be treated with nothing but scorn because the child was to blame. The reason her love had abandoned her. Had been driven away…

He wouldn't cause another woman's unhappiness.

Raffaele disposed of the condom in the bin and opened the door, moved through it. His feet were taking him back to her. He needed to tell her—fix this. Protect her. *Himself.*

He walked back into the bedroom.

Everything stood still. Stopped.

She was gone.

Naked, he moved through the hallway, went back to the lounge, opened every door, flicked every switch, turned on every light. He paused only for a moment to pull on his underwear before jogging out onto the terrace. He moved to the concealed door, yanked it open, took the steps to the floor beneath two at a time.

She was nowhere.

Gone.

He ran to the elevator at the end of the corridor. He jabbed at the buttons. His gut demanded he go and knock on every door. Wake up whoever was inside and demand if they housed her.

But he wouldn't.

The lift arrived. He threw himself inside and hit the buttons. All of them. He dragged his fingers through his hair. If she had a room…if she was still in the hotel…he would find her. He had to tell her.

With each stop of the elevator he stepped outside, searched the quiet halls on every floor with his eyes. The emptiness was so loud his ears ached.

The lift doors pinged for the last time and opened to an empty reception area. His chest heaved. He strode forward. Stood still in the centre of the grand foyer. Raised his head to the chandelier and stained-glass ceiling and took in the hotel's hugeness.

His hotel.

Twenty floors. Four hundred and thirty-seven rooms. Fifteen more hidden rooms adjoining secret stairs and hidden exits. Possibly hundreds of occupants in the entire hotel…thousands of names…

He wanted to roar. Demand her presence. But he did not know her name, this anonymous woman who might have a piece of him growing inside her.

The image of a boy no more than five flashed in his mind. Alone. Kicked out of his house by his mother, screaming for him to get out. Telling him that she didn't want him. That she never had. Lonely and afraid, the little boy had left. Because he didn't know how to make his mother happy. How to keep the fridge full. How to make her *want* him.

His child would never be unwanted.

It would always be aware of who it was and where it came from.

His child would not only survive—it would thrive. With *his* name and the empire he'd built around it. His child would know it had a place in this world. His child would be protected.

If she was pregnant.

Whatever it took—*however long it took*—he would find her...

CHAPTER THREE

Six weeks later...

RAFFAELE GRIPPED THE CONTROLS. The view before him was a patchwork quilt of dull green, with black shadows of gnarly trees dotting the hills and dips of the English countryside. Ancient woodlands, shaped and bent by the coastal winds at his back, bowed to him as he flew past. His helicopter sliced through the lavender streaks of a determined sun, turning the grey mist lingering in the air into a display of contrasts.

For six weeks she'd lived in his head.

Finding her had been more difficult than he'd expected because she hadn't used her real name to book into the hotel.

She'd used her birth name.

Flora Campbell. Abandoned into the care system at fourteen weeks old. Remained in the foster system until two farmers adopted her and whisked her away to a dairy farm straddling the borders of two villages housing only a few thousand people.

He'd grown up in a village, too—of sorts. An untouched wilderness in the eastern hills of Sicily. Too far away from the coastal towns to attract tourists, too wild for the civilised.

It had been a small community who'd often noticed a young boy out alone at night. Who'd whispered among themselves that if that boy whose mother lived in the house on top of the hill, who told stories of a count who lived in castles and who was coming back to claim her as soon as he'd left his wife, was wandering lost and alone you sent him back home with some food.

Because that boy lived with a woman so deep in her depression that the villagers knew his whereabouts before his mother did.

Without them he—

Raffaele thrust the memories aside. He'd survived largely on his own. Strangers' generosity had filled his belly when the money hidden under the bed had run out, but he'd always been an outcast. On the periphery. Having to rely on himself. And he'd made it on his own.

He'd scrimped and he'd saved to buy his first renovation project. An abandoned house in the village. He'd pulled it apart and put it back together. Brick by brick. And then he'd posted it online, imploring tourists to flock to it and take pretty pictures of his renovations. Then he'd sold it. And then he'd done it again. Until a one-man band had become a crew. A business. An international multi-billion-dollar company.

But there was no time to think about that now. Because every time he'd closed his eyes since that night it had not been his mother's face he'd seen. It had been *hers*. Flora Campbell. Flora Bick.

Raffaele pulled the helicopter to a hovering halt above a snow-speckled field. Anticipation feathered over his skin. His team had delivered more than her adopted name. He had an address. Details of her routines—the farm's routines. Knew the fields they used for wildflowers to encourage nature. And which were the kale fields...the fields full of turnips for the livestock to graze, or something or other. He didn't care. Only wanted to know that it was safe to land— and it was.

He circled the fields in a three-hundred-and-sixty-degree turn, found the field marked with an X in his mind's eye, and descended. It was the only destination he'd thought of for six entire weeks.

He was making his way back to *her*.

And if she was pregnant there was only one choice to be made.

She wouldn't run again. He'd tether them together for the sake of his child.

They'd be bound by law and marriage.

Flora was tired. The fatigue running through her mind and body was so intense it was bone-deep. She'd fallen back into the farm's routine as if her night alone in London hadn't happened and her life had resumed as normal.

But her body hadn't forgotten.

It remembered…

For one night there had been no alarm set for morning milking. No routine to maintain. With him, she hadn't been a farm hand, nor the abandoned daughter of an addict. She'd been a woman. Free to explore herself when she'd never been given a voice. Never been allowed to use her words without checking them first in her head for fear of hurting those who loved her.

He hadn't known her. He hadn't even known her name. Her actions on that one occasion wouldn't give strength to her parents' worries for their adopted child. Her compulsive nature couldn't hurt *him*. So the rules hadn't applied. There had been no rigid expectations.

But going off the script, allowing the intensity of her feelings to take root, had overwhelmed her.

So she'd run. Back to her life. To what she

knew. Because she wasn't *that* woman. Not in real life. Not now the haze of pleasure had faded. She didn't know how to be *her*. The possibility of staying longer in his bed and letting herself explore that woman in his arms had terrified her.

But he'd awoken her body in London, and her body couldn't forget the change he'd brought about in her. She felt restless. She felt...*restricted*.

A heavy, dull sound reverberated in her ears. She knew all the sounds on the farm. And the times they occurred. The low hum of the milking parlour, the deep trumpeting sound of the cows, the tick of the tractors. Most of all, she knew the stillness. The quiet. But there was no longer silence.

The air hummed with something unknown.

Something imminent.

And it was getting louder.

Closer.

Flora slipped off her yellow rubber gloves, placed them on the draining board, and followed the noise outside.

Everything looked the same as it always did.

She'd stood in this exact spot many times. With the gravel beneath her feet, the farmhouse to her back, the stone drive in front of her leading to more fields and to roads that hadn't made it on to a map.

Only this time there was a shadow amongst the snowy fields. A mountainous man in a black suit.

Him.

Flora tugged her bottom lip between her teeth and pressed down, stemming the roar of something deep inside her...the part of her that recognised him.

And all six feet plus of masculine energy was charging towards her.

He crossed the field in the sun he'd brought with him. It pierced through the broken clouds, highlighting the black curls kissing his earlobes.

Goosebumps prickled to life on Flora's arms, beneath her woollen jumper. She swallowed. He was as out of place as a city high-rise in the middle of a field. With a helicopter at his back. He didn't belong here. But excitement sang to life inside her. Her pulse became a frantic beat.

He'd tracked her down...

Why?

He stopped before her, filling the air with the scent of him. Something deeply male. Uniquely him. Masculine. But it seemed different. *He* seemed different. Restrained inside his suit...

'Piccolina...'

That word. A word she didn't know the meaning of, but he'd given it to her. An unknown name for a temporary woman.

But she wasn't that woman now.

She was Flora Bick, daughter of farmers. An adoptee. A miracle baby saved from the hands of her maternal mother.

'How did you find me?' she whispered. The sound of her voice was foreign. Husky.

'Did you not want to be found?'

The seams of his jacket tightened on his shoulders, bulging under the strain of his muscles as they moved. And she wanted to touch them.

She curled her hands into tight fists to stop herself from reaching out.

'We said no names,' she reminded him as flashes of the woman she'd been with him entered her consciousness. Her slipping off the straps of her dress, presenting herself to him…

No. That wasn't the woman she'd been trained to be. She wasn't spontaneous. She didn't push against the invisible walls around her. She stood exactly where she was told to stand. To sit. To eat. To stay.

When they'd shared that night together she'd been someone else.

And those two women did not align.

They could not co-exist.

'We said many things,' he said, interrupting her racing justification of who she was…who she'd allowed herself to be with him. 'And things changed.'

'Changed…?' Her eyes travelled over the taut

lines of his clean-shaven cheeks to the pulse that pounded there. '*Nothing* has changed,' she said.

Because it hadn't for her. Their time together lived in the shadows of her mind, not in the broad light of day.

'Has it not?' His eyes blazed, a colour she still couldn't name. Burned into her with every caress of his gaze along her skin. And he didn't rush. He took in every detail.

She shook her head, her heart racing. 'No. Nothing has changed,' she repeated—because it hadn't. Not for her. She'd gone back to her life. Back to her risk-free existence.

There were no choices now. She could be only one woman here. The person her parents needed her to be. The only person she truly knew how to be.

His eyes flicked back to her face. 'Nothing?'

An unwavering confidence exuded from his every pore, and Flora couldn't help feeling that he knew something she didn't. His gaze pulled at something inside her. Something she'd buried deep.

Her breath hitched, stuttering in the chilly morning air and burning away into dew on the heat of her parted lips.

Because something had changed.

In a world where she wasn't allowed to keep her own secrets, she had one.

Her night with him had been a forbidden erotic salute to her DNA. To the part of herself that she couldn't allow. And she didn't want to give it any more freedom than one night, those few hours. Otherwise satisfying her own needs, her own desire, might consume her.

The way it had consumed her mother.

'How did you find me?' she asked, ignoring the desire ripping through her to ask *why* he'd found her.

She'd left no traces of Flora Bick. She'd checked in to the hotel under her birth name and she'd left Flora Campbell behind in London.

And yet here he was.

The presence of him filled the stillness. The quiet. And it was loud, demanding her attention. She couldn't stop looking at him and remembering the choices she had made with him.

She suppressed the shiver threatening to crawl across her skin and clenched her fists tighter. Afraid that she'd reach out and touch him. Test the reality of him in the light of day.

'The way I find anything,' he answered, slicing through her thoughts and dragging her gaze back to his.

He stepped towards her, shortening the space between them, stealing the air she was trying to inhale and replacing it with something visceral. Something new, something *possessive*, that reached across the distance between them.

'I hunt.'

A helpless sound left her lips. 'I'm not an animal,' she said, because it terrified her. *Excited* her. His words hit her stomach in rush of need. Ignited an instant hunger inside her to be claimed. *Found.* 'You can't hunt human beings.'

'And yet here I am,' he corrected her. 'Having hunted *you*.'

He'd been a ghost in her life…reminding her of her past, that she was an addict's daughter. Reminding her of how easily she'd given in to her compulsions. And here he was now. Reminding her of the kissing, the touching, the *freedom* she'd felt in his arms. How she'd acted no better than an animal driven by need.

But she was not her biological mother. She might be susceptible to addiction, but she could resist, couldn't she? She had to. She wouldn't give in to her body's demands again. She would control her impulses. This instant and all-consuming pull to touch him could and would be held at bay.

'I should go back inside,' she said.

He placed a hand on her hip. Gently. But she was rooted to the spot by the heat radiating from his palm, infiltrating the layers of clothes covering her skin.

He swallowed thickly, the taut lines in his throat stretching. 'Do not run from me again.'

It was a command, but a pleading note punctuated it.

Flora couldn't do anything but plant her feet to the ground. The danger was standing right in front of her, touching her, but she couldn't shrug off his hold on her body because his fingers on her jean-clad hip weren't what was holding her in place. It was the intensity in his eyes.

'I didn't run the first time,' she lied, because she couldn't confess the truth. 'I walked straight out through the front door of the hotel.'

He pulled his hand away. 'Without saying goodbye?'

Shame gripped her. Quietly, she'd slipped from his room and gone back to her own. She'd collected the folder containing the redacted version of her life and then she'd run all the way home. From bus to train. City to country. From field to farm. Ready to fall back into line. Obey the rules. Forget everything she'd learnt in London.

She'd locked her time in London away…justified her reckless actions as being just one night. One slip from grace.

She wouldn't slip again.

'Why would I say goodbye when we didn't say hello?'

'We shared—'

'A night. A moment,' she interrupted. 'And you're not following the rules.'

'Rules?'

'Of one-night stands.'

He raised a dark brow sardonically. 'You'd know because you've had so many?'

She clamped down on her bottom lip. He was scribbling outside the lines on purpose. While she was trying to stay within them with painstaking determination.

But it clawed through her. The realisation that she wanted to break the rules, too. She wanted to stem the itch on her palm by placing it on his cheek, to see how smooth his skin was without the stubble he'd had all those weeks ago. She wanted to run her fingers along his jaw, to stare into his eyes and demand he kiss her. *Everywhere.* She didn't want to be this woman who lived to make others happy. She wanted to be free.

One more time.

Flora shut those thoughts down and looked at him. Tried to concentrate on the black suit sheathing his muscles and the leather shoes cushioning his feet. On anything but how he made her feel. Chaotic. Unsteady. When her life had always been so balanced and so sheltered.

'You have no right to be here,' she said, stamping down on the idea that he might have found her again because he wanted to extend their night. To claim her again.

'I have every right,' he contradicted her.

She shook her head and the messy bun piled on top of her head wobbled, strands of hair falling around her face.

He raised his long fingers to her cheek, and she held her breath as he caught a tendril between his thumb and forefinger and tucked it behind her ear. 'You are coming undone, *piccolina*.'

'Undone?' she echoed.

'Unravelling,' he confirmed, his voice a sultry caress to the heavy weight in her chest.

Throatily, she repeated her earlier question. 'Why are you here?' She shouldn't care. But she did. She wanted and she needed to know.

Softly, his fingers wrapped around her wrist. 'Can you not guess?'

Heat penetrated her skin. Not a trickle, not a seeping warmth, but a shot of hotness directly into her veins.

'No…' She swallowed thickly. Her throat was too dry.

'Guess,' he urged her, his eyes fixed on her face. 'Why would a man you spent the night with seek you out? *Hunt* you?'

His words were gentle. Inviting. Coaxing her to tell him a secret she didn't have access to. She felt trapped. He was a hunter moving in on his prey, ready to pounce.

'Don't play with me,' she said. 'Why are you here?'

'Because I need to know.'

'Know *what*?' She breathed the words, low and long.

'Are you or are you not?' he asked.

'Am I or am I not what?'

'Pregnant.'

'Pregnant?'

In that moment, everything stilled. Went blank. Before it all collided. Every memory of her safe and predictable life and her night with him. 'What?'

'Are you or are you not pregnant,' he confirmed, his voice a low husk of possession.

Her gaze turned fuzzy around the edges. A huge shadow wobbled before her eyes. *Him.* The mountain of a man she'd chosen to give herself to.

What had she done?

The air, hot and pulsing, from her lips swirled together and pushed out a question. 'You're talking about a baby?'

He gave a single nod.

And Flora fainted.

CHAPTER FOUR

'HAVE YOU EATEN?'

Flora ignored the voice, somewhere distant but somehow close almost in her ear. She wasn't hungry. She was warm. *Toasty.* She snuggled closer to the source, pressing her nose against something soft and hard at the same time.

There was a touch. Something gentle stroking at her forehead. Lulling her into awareness… into consciousness.

Her eyes flew open and there was the world looking back at her. Swirls of green and blue and vivid streaks of grey.

Her gut clenched. Reality was trying to push at her senses too rapidly for her to catch anything coherent.

She was cocooned in the embrace of his body, sitting in his lap. In his arms. Her neck was resting in the crook of his elbow as he stared down at her—

Pregnant.

She scrambled out of his arms and into the seat beside him. She looked over the field to her house and then back at him.

'Did you carry me across the field?'

'I don't know who's inside.' His broad shoulder dipped. 'I didn't want to shock them.'

'It must be handy, having a portable spaceship to haul damsels in distress to safety.'

The smile she'd intended to put on her lips never appeared, because her joke wasn't funny. None of this was funny.

'It's the easiest form of transport,' he said, not acknowledging her attempt at…at what? Humour?

'I suppose so…'

She straightened, pressing her back against the hard leather. The helicopter doors were open. The cab was big and there were two rows of seating behind the flight deck. But he filled them. Long legs outstretched, his body was turned towards her, his knees a millimetre from touching hers.

'Have you eaten?' he repeated.

'No.' She pulled her knees together, placed her sweaty palms down on her thighs, refused to drag them over her jeans to remove the sweat. 'I'm sorry I fainted. I don't faint. Have never fainted before.'

'It was a shock? Finding out that you might

be pregnant?' She heard it, the dip in his voice making his response a question.

She nodded, and she forget to exhale, because he seemed to get bigger. His shoulders widened as he leaned into the inhalation of breath.

His eyes skirted to the left briefly and then shot back to hers. 'What do you usually eat for breakfast?'

'Porridge,' she answered absently.

'You need to eat.'

'Why are you talking about food?' Her nose pinched as a wave of nausea crawled up her throat. 'You don't have to feed me up. I'm not pregnant,' she declared. 'I can't be.' But her bottom lip wobbled.

'You know this as a certainty?' His gaze burned into her. Diving inside her. Seeking secrets. Seeking answers. Answers she didn't have.

'We used protection...'

As rapidly as a fire spreading after receiving a gust of oxygen he was on his phone, blasting out a long stream of words that were foreign to her. But there was no doubting that it was a series of commands that he spoke into the mouthpiece, while never taking his eyes off her.

Slipping the phone back into his inside pocket, he shook his head. 'You *could* be pregnant,' he corrected.

His voice was a low husk of possession, and it

reached across the distance between them. This was surreal... *Impossible!* Her life was scripted. Planned. Her days followed a routine down to the minute.

After London—after collecting the file and discovering the truth of her adoption—she'd returned to her life because it was safe And predictable. But she'd been unable to hide from all the questions in her head, from the intensity of what she'd felt.

The night she'd met him she hadn't had to think. She'd operated on autopilot, supressing her emotions, never allowing them to overwhelm her. She hadn't needed to be anything other than the woman she knew she could be. She'd managed to lock everything away.

Only now it all threatened to spill out, to escape. And she wasn't ready for that. She had to be able to think clearly.

'I'm *not* pregnant.' She swallowed convulsively. 'We—*you*—used protection. I saw—'

Her body tightened deep down inside as the memory of the pleasure of feeling him pushing inside her flooded her brain. Her senses.

'The condom tore,' he told her, his tone matter-of-fact. Unemotional. Toneless.

Rapid and shallow, her breathing picked up pace. 'Tore...?'

He moved then. Slid himself along the seat

until there was no more than an inch between them. Their knees knocked, and it took all of her concentration not to inhale the scent of soap and clean cotton. Of *him*. The scent was something so familiar and yet so unknown that it was as terrifying as it was exciting.

'If you hadn't run,' he said, 'I would have told you that night.'

It was like a punch to the gut. Flora closed her eyes. Breathed in through her nose and out through her mouth. 'I… I was afraid,' she confessed, opening her eyes to meet his unwavering steady gaze.

'Of me?' he asked, his voice deep. Gravelly.

She shook her head and swallowed thickly. 'Couldn't you feel it?' she whispered.

A deep furrow appeared between his eyebrows. 'Feel what?'

A blush crawled up her throat. What was the point of lying? He was here, and her decision to run had affected them both. Pulled them out of their dreamlike encounter into reality. Into her real life. Why shouldn't she ask all the questions that had plagued her for weeks? About her reaction to him? About her body's response to his touch.

She pressed her palms to her thighs and told him the truth. 'The temptation to do it all over again.'

The vein in his throat became more pronounced as he asked, 'This frightened you?' His eyes narrowed. 'Because I hurt you?'

'No, the pain was minimal. But the pleasure was…' She hesitated. 'It was all-consuming. It was too intense, too frantic, and I… I was afraid that what you'd awoken inside me would never go back to sleep if I stayed for a second longer in your bed.'

His fingers flexed at his sides. 'You ran because you were afraid of who you were with me?'

'Yes.' She blew out a shaky breath between pursed lips.

Eyes narrowed, he nodded.

'Is it always like that?' she asked, because a part of her really wanted to know. 'Sex?' she clarified. 'Is it always so…intoxicating?'

The idea that he might have tracked her down simply because he wanted her was distant. Was she naïve to think a man would seek her out because the sex had been *that* good?

But she *was* naïve, wasn't she? Had been sheltered from life on purpose. Wrapped in cotton wool so she didn't accidentally discover that her biological mother had a disease that might live inside her too, deep in her genetic make-up.

His eyes darkened. 'No.'

'Was it like that for you too?'

Did it matter?

She didn't know. Only that she wanted the answer. 'With me?' she asked.

'I...' He faltered. The pulse in his cheek hammered. 'That is not important. Not right now. What is important is that it has been six weeks,' he said. 'Time enough for your body to tell you if there have been consequences of the pleasure you were so afraid of, *piccolina*.' He paused before continuing. 'Has your period arrived?' he asked,

But the question wasn't filled with recrimination or accusation. He wanted the facts. Facts she was still trying to put in order. It didn't make sense. None of it.

Heat crept into her cheeks. Maybe she hadn't been listening to her body. Maybe she had been too busy trying to slip back into her life to listen.

Her hands moved to rest on her flat stomach. 'I don't *feel* pregnant,' she said, more to herself than to him.

She looked down at her hands, at the makeshift cradle she'd created around her stomach. Her body still felt like hers. Not a host to a new life.

'We will take a test,' he said.

Flora snapped her gaze back to his. 'You have brought a pregnancy test with you?'

'Unfortunately I don't keep pregnancy tests in my breast pocket,' he said.

Her breath shuddered in her chest. Was this his attempt at humour?

'But I've purchased one.'

'Where is it?' she asked.

'It will be waiting for us at my home.'

'Us?' she repeated. She'd never been part of an *us*.

'I can't do it without you,' he said, closing his mouth and watching her watch him.

'No, I suppose you can't,' she agreed. 'But why is someone taking a test to your house when you're here, in my home? With me?'

'It was the easier choice,' he dismissed, without further explanation.

'But we're *here*…' she pressed.

'And soon we will be *there*,' he countered, matter-of-factly.

'How did you find me?' she asked, brows knitted. He hadn't answered her before. 'Did you hire a private investigator?'

'A team of them,' he replied, without so much as a blush.

She pointed a trembling finger at his chest. 'You read all the files on me?'

'How else was I to find you?'

'You weren't *supposed* to find me.'

She dropped her hand into her lap and raised

her gaze to the ceiling. It felt like a betrayal. He'd so easily summoned information on her when she'd had to wait twenty-one years to learn about Flora Campbell.

She looked at him. 'I didn't want to remember.'

His eyes flashed, his pupils growing larger. 'There's no forgetting now.'

Flora looked at him—at this man who'd given her a taste of life outside the farm—and she recognised that some part of her had wanted that night, and him, to stay separate from her real life. Her farm life. Something to remind her that there was magic in plain sight if she pushed to look for it.

'I might *not* be pregnant,' she reminded him. And herself.

'But if you are I insist our child will know its roots. Its beginnings. Its biological parents. I will not leave it to think it is unwanted. That there is no one to protect it. Because I will claim it. I will want it.'

'How dare you use what you've read about me to bring me on side?'

His eyes narrowed. 'Why do you assume it is *your* past that guides me? I am not trying to manipulate you. I have come to you, I have found you, and I have offered you facts. We will discover if there are consequences together. Now you must trust me.'

Her head spun. 'Trust you…?'

'Trust me to navigate the next steps.'

'The next steps…?'

Flora closed her eyes briefly. What was she? A parrot? If she *was* pregnant, where would that leave her? Single? But tied to a man she'd given her virginity to for the rest of her life simply because a condom had split?

'What choice do you have, *piccolina*?' His features did not move. Not even a flicker. 'We will leave here now and do a test together.'

'What if I am pregnant—?'

'First,' he interrupted, 'we will find out if you are.'

'And if I am?' she pushed. Because this was her life, and she was tired of facts being withheld from her. Of finding out after everyone else.

'We'll get married, of course.'

'Married?' she repeated, because so easily had the word fallen from his mouth. As easily as the news that she might be carrying his child. She wasn't finding any of those words easy. 'Why?'

'If you are pregnant with my child, the child also belongs to me. I protect what is mine.'

'A baby's not a possession. You can't claim ownership. Pass it around like an unwanted pet—'

'Would you have preferred that I left you to

discover this on your own? That I left you to struggle with single motherhood?'

'I *am* single,' she reminded him.

His lips compressed. 'Not any more.'

'You can't claim me just because you will it,' she said, dismissing his possessive claim with a wave of her unsteady hand.

'If you are pregnant,' he said, 'our baby deserves to know where it comes from. *Who* it comes from. It has a right to its father's name. *My* name.'

There was something in his tone—something raw. As though he'd revealed too much.

'Are those your own words?'

She bit hard on her lower lip. Words were swimming in her head. *Pregnant. A baby. Failure. A mistake. Discovered and abandoned. Unwanted.*

'Or words you've taken and recycled from my file? Did you read that my biological father is unknown to me?'

'I did.' His eyes darkened. 'And I too understand—*intimately*—the weight of being denied your true origins.'

'You were adopted too?' she asked, her brain jumping quickly to that conclusion.

'No. But I lived only with my mother, who told me stories of my father being a count. Italian nobility.'

His tone was flat and sober as he told her this, giving nothing away.

'He'd hidden her away for the shame of having his illegitimate son.'

'You're the illegitimate son?'

'I am,' he confirmed.

'Did it hurt?'

'Which bit?'

'The stories?' she asked.

She'd never know who her biological father was, and that would always leave a hole inside her. But at least she hadn't been soothed by stories of a father who might be aristocracy to lessen the blow.

'Until I reached twenty-one my parents told me stories too,' she said. 'Not as wild as having nobility for parents. But never the facts. Never the truth.'

'What kind of stories?'

'Stories to hide the reasons why I was home-schooled. The reasons I shouldn't follow my instincts but plan and execute carefully designed routines, so I didn't ever become consumed by my passions.'

'Why would they do that?'

'I have an addictive personality. I focus on things…' she shrugged, tugging her bottom lip between her teeth '…and I fixate.'

'What things do you focus on?'

'Fixing things, usually…' She paused, feeling a tightness that was making it difficult to form a placating smile. Making it difficult to swallow.

He shrugged. 'Focusing—*prioritising*—in a world full of noise is a skill, not a fault.'

'Maybe…' she conceded.

'Is that why you think you don't know yourself? Because you were never told your truth? Your story?' he asked, and with that he catapulted her six weeks into the past.

'You remember?'

'I remember everything.'

And so did she. Every caress of his fingers. Every touch of his—

She pushed them down. The memories. And she ignored the heavy drag in her stomach.

'I'm their miracle baby,' she said, as if that would explain everything. And to her it did.

'I was an unwanted bastard,' he answered. 'And you were a miracle. Two opposite ends of the spectrum. No child of mine will never be a mistake. My child will never be a bastard. Never unwanted or illegitimate,' he bit out between tight lips. 'If you are pregnant, our baby will always know where it belongs. That it is protected. Safe.'

His eyes held hers with an intensity so strong she could feel the pulse of it in her chest.

'With me,' he said.

'You weren't safe?' she asked, feeling a stab of something visceral to her solar plexus. 'When you were growing up?'

'I grew up in the eastern hills of Sicily. It's…' he frowned '…beautiful. Untouched and out of the way of things. If we'd lived closer to the coastal towns, to people who might have seen my mother's illness—'

'Your mother was ill?'

'Mentally ill. To the point where she couldn't function.'

She watched his Adam's apple drag up and down his taut throat.

'Or care for a little boy who was hungry more often than not.'

'You don't want the same for you child?' she said. 'That's why you're here? Because—?'

'Exactly.' His gaze locked on her stomach. 'My child will not be hungry. My child will never be cold.'

Connection surged between them. Not like the night they'd met. Something deeper. Something she couldn't name or place. But she recognised it was happening.

'Did your mother tell you stories of Italian nobility because she didn't know who your father was? Or did she tell you them because she didn't want to tell you the truth?'

'Some of my mother's stories were true…

some false,' he answered. 'I only found out which when I was much older, and then it didn't matter to me any more what was fiction or fact. I'd grown up without a father...without his name. All I knew was that we were hungry and that my mother had been abandoned by a man who didn't want to claim either her or me. He paid her off with a wad of cash that lived under the bed in a jar until it was all gone. He left us in a village where they called my mother—'

He looked away, at the floor, and she felt the rawness of his vulnerability.

He raised his head, his face an emotionless mask of beauty. 'But she knew who my father was.'

'So it's true?' she asked, eyes wide. 'Your father's an Italian count?'

'He is—*was*,' he corrected. 'My father is dead.'

'When did he die?'

'Six months ago.'

'And your mum?'

'Three months ago.'

'Oh...so much death...'

Her throat constricted. And yet they might have made life in all the grief.

She swallowed. Shook herself. 'I'm so sorry.'

'I didn't know my father.' He blinked slowly. 'I didn't grieve for him. I didn't *need* my father, or his name. But I deserved it. And you deserve to know *my* name, Flora.'

Her name on his lips was too real. It brought their night together, their future, to the real world of names and consequences. Actions and reactions. Negatives and positives.

'I am Ra—'

'No!' she pleaded, palms forward. 'I'm not ready. Please, don't tell me your name.'

Nostrils flaring, he asked, 'Why not?'

'If—' Her tongue grappled with words, refusing to organise them inside her mouth. 'If you tell me your name you become real,' she said, trying to explain. '*This* becomes real,' she concluded, her hands splayed in front of her chest.

'This *is* real.' His eyes probed her face but he didn't move. Not a muscle. '*I'm* real.'

And that was the problem, wasn't it? He was being honest about his life and so was she—for the first time. There she sat in a helicopter, in the middle of a field, with a man she'd never been supposed to see again.

But none of it would matter if she wasn't pregnant. This intensity, this sense of being overwhelmed, this influx of emotion that so terrified her would be temporary.

She opened her eyes. 'I'll come with you,' she said, deciding to be honest. Because why not after all he'd shared with her about his mother? His illegitimacy? 'Under one condition.'

'What is it?'

'That you don't tell me your name unless I'm pregnant. Because if I'm not pregnant, none of this will matter.'

He nodded. 'I will remain a stranger to you until we become something else,' he promised, the pulse flickering wildly in his cheek.

'If,' she corrected. 'If we become something else.'

His eyes flashed and her stomach flipped, and the *'we'* lingered in the air.

And then, just as he had that night, he offered her his hand.

A rush of excitement—or was it fear, perhaps?—pulsed through her veins in waves.

Tentatively she slid her fingers between his and he claimed her hand, lifting her out of the helicopter to pull her into step beside him. He opened the door to the flight deck, nodded towards the co-pilot's seat.

Flora climbed inside. His hands were on her waist, guiding her. He buckled her in and then climbed in himself, buckled himself into the pilot's seat.

He flicked a switch on the dashboard, handed her a headset. She mimicked him as he put his own on, sliding it on her head and pulling down the mouthpiece even though she knew they were out of words. There was nothing left to say.

The helicopter blades spun furiously and pulled them up into the air. Away from the farm. Away from everything she'd ever known.

Flora realised that she wasn't leaving as Flora Campbell, the abandoned daughter of an addict. But neither was she Flora Bick, a miracle baby adopted by farmers. She was leaving as a potential mother…and maybe someone's soon-to-be wife.

His wife.

She'd have to learn a whole new script—a brand-new list of rules for a completely different life where she'd decide how she lived it. Who she wanted to be.

And if the time came to make a choice, who would she choose?

CHAPTER FIVE

THE HELICOPTER SWOOPED between the coastal cliffs and out over the open sea straight towards a white and blue vessel. A boat—a *yacht*—of magnificent proportions.

Flora's skin prickled. She turned her head, looking back towards the beach. She *knew* that beach. Combed it regularly for shells, or driftwood, for signs of life outside the farm. But she'd dragged nothing back to the farm as large as *him*.

She turned back to him…the man who was piloting the helicopter. Was it *his* helicopter?

Her temples pounded with the realisation of that. Surely if they were having a baby together that was information she should know? But she didn't. She'd been too swept up in the other revelations of the last hour. His return. The failed contraception. The potential pregnancy. A baby…

Suddenly a barrage of images slammed

against her brain. *The helicopter. The suit. The roof. The opulent rooms at the hotel!* Her eyes snapped to the view in front of them, focusing on the yacht…a water palace. She'd been blinded by emotion, by passion. She hadn't seen what was right in front of her.

He lowered the helicopter onto the tail-end of the yacht, onto a helipad. Flora held her breath during the descent. He was a man of means, wasn't he? A man who'd been able to find her when she'd barely been able to find out any information about herself for herself. He'd hired a team of private investigators…

'The hotel…'

She hesitated as he flicked some switches. Turned off a blinking light and removed his headset. The whir of the helicopter propellers slowed to a gentle buzz.

Did she truly want to know more about the man who could be the father of her child? Did she want to make this real before they confirmed the consequences? Did she need to?

Before Flora could swallow he was getting out, walking around the front of the helicopter to appear on her side. He pulled open her door and stood there expectantly. The sea stretched out behind him, calm, and a new world of opulence surrounded the helicopter. Gleaming glass and polished silver rails were stacked in rows, on top of one another, which she could only assume signified more decks, more rooms...

'I'm not getting out.'

He cocked a brow. 'You're not?'

She shook her head so violently that she dislodged her headset. She caught it. 'No, I'm not.'

How could she when she didn't know what kind of world she was stepping into. She'd hadn't considered it before. She'd been too focused on finding out if she was pregnant, never stopping to question where he'd be taking her. Where his home was.

He took the headset from her hands, his fingers brushing the tips of hers.

No. She wouldn't look at his hands. She wouldn't recognise the jolt in her stomach for what it was. Because desire was intoxicating. *Consuming.* She needed facts—not emotion. She must not let herself be swayed by these addictive feelings.

She needed not to recognise the sensations in her stomach, and lower, that the single caress of his hand against hers had caused. Because it was ludicrous how badly she wanted him when she still didn't know who he was. This stranger— this man—the potential father of her potential baby...

He threw the headset onto the dashboard. 'Why not?' Amusement laced his voice.

Flora inhaled deeply through her nostrils and squared her shoulders, steeling herself. She'd let her emotions overrule logic. With him, she'd ignored every lesson ingrained by her parents to call for rational thinking before impulse. Now she needed information. She needed to be able to think clearly.

'Tell me who you are?' she demanded tightly.

He narrowed his eyes. 'Why is it important now?'

'Because I don't think your world is anything like mine. I think—*I thought* the man on that rooftop was staying in the hotel, like me. He just had a better room with a better view. But you *own* that view, don't you?'

'What do you mean?'

'I need to know who you are,' she repeated. 'I need to know the facts. *Now.*'

'I have no problem telling you who I am. You were the one who wished not to know my name—'

'I was wrong,' she admitted. 'The truth is that this is real—whether or not I want to acknowledge it. I can't hide from it because here we are…'

She raised her hands and gesticulated to the view. To the sea surrounding them at every turn.

'I want to find out if I'm pregnant knowing all the facts. *Real* facts. I want to rip off the blindfold that's been obscuring the view my whole life and go into this with my eyes wide open. I owe it to any potential child to know who I might've made it with.' She sucked in a breath. 'And don't we owe it to ourselves?'

'Of course,' he agreed. 'We deserve to have each other's names.'

'Then tell me yours.'

'I am Raffaele Russo. CEO of Russo Renovations. Sicilian born and bred. Multi-billionaire.'

He closed the distance even between them and, his mouth a whisper's breadth from her own, said, 'I am the father of the potential baby who potentially grows inside you.'

Desire pulsed between them even now, throwing her the absurd image of herself leaning in and pressing her mouth to his.

She shook it off.

'Billionaire?' she repeated, and pulled back enough so that she couldn't taste the warmth of his breath on her lips.

'*Multi*-billionaire,' he corrected.

'But you said you grew up in the middle of nowhere. That your mother couldn't afford heating. How did you make so much money?'

Eyes hooded, he asked, 'Does it matter?'

'Of course it does. Why didn't you tell me you were rich?'

'You never asked.'

Of course she hadn't. How could she ever have imagined herself to exist in the same world as a billionaire? To be desired by a billionaire? How could she ever have imagined that a billionaire wanted her? A woman who had no idea where she really came from…

'And you never thought to say?' she asked,

What did this mean? For her? For her potential child?

Raffaele shrugged. 'I'm comfortable with the man I am. There is no need to flaunt my existence.'

There was more to it—she could tell by the casual way he threw the comment out into the world. There was no time to dwell on that. But was Flora comfortable with it?

'Tell me how you became a billionaire?' she asked.

'I won't romanticise the past. It was hard. Scarlata is small.'

'Scarlata?'

'My village. Only a hundred people. It didn't have access to many things, but it had access to the outside world. A connection to the internet. For the posting of the kind of pretty pictures people like to post on social media.'

'What do pretty pictures on social media have to do with anything?'

'Pretty pictures make money.'

Her brain couldn't connect the dots. 'I don't understand…'

He smiled, but his eyes didn't. Shadows played inside them and she couldn't make out their shape.

'You don't like pretty pictures, *piccolina*?'

'Why?' She smiled tentatively. 'Are you a photographer?'

'I'm a builder,' he said. 'I build things. Fix things. But back then I found an old digital camera on a farm on the outskirts of the village.'

'There was a farm?'

'They made cheese there for three generations and sold it to the big cities. Tourists didn't visit my village, but they visited the farm online, to watch, and I watched them.'

'You lived on a farm?' she asked, her heart absurdly lifting at the idea that he'd grown up in a place exactly like her.

He shook his head. 'I helped there sometimes, because they gave me cheese and bread enough to feed my *mamma*. To feed myself. But tourists need more than bread dipped in cheese. More than pasta and tomatoes. Tourists need a place to go. They've seen the pretty pictures online. They need a place to sleep.'

'You gave them a bed?'

'No. I built them one.'

'You built them a place to sleep?'

'Where do *you* sleep, Flora?'

'In a bed…'

'Where did the bed come from?'

'A shop.'

'Where did the shop get the bed?'

She frowned. 'From a bed-maker…?'

'Exactly.' He applauded without sound, pressing his palms together. 'Well done.'

'No need to patronise me.'

'I'm not,' he placated. 'Where I'm from, there weren't the commodities you have in your village. If I needed something the only option was to travel to one of the major towns or big cities to get it, or to build it myself. I didn't have the means to travel, so I built things. And I traded for them. I traded my physical strength for a meal. The work of my hands…'

He held them out in front of him and her eyes snapped to them. To the calluses on his palms that would never heal. She remembered their slight roughness against her hips as he'd held her in place and devoured—

'These hands,' he continued, 'wrapped parcels of cheese for seven days straight without sleep. Because I wanted to learn—to listen—to understand what those tourists were doing and to figure out how I could make money from them.'

'How *did* you make money from them?'

'I flipped an abandoned house in the centre

of the village, in the middle of everything—near the local shop, the café and the bar—and turned it into a rustic den of opulence. A two-floor haven. Using materials hidden in basements of the local community.'

'The community?'

'They…helped me.'

She heard it. The croak of distaste.

'I'm glad someone did,' she whispered. 'I'm glad someone helped you.'

'It was a long time ago,' he dismissed. 'I don't need help any more. But if I learnt anything from living in the middle of nowhere, I learned two things. If you climb up, you hold your hand out for the next person. You protect your own. *I protect my own.*'

His voice was fierce—animated—and she sat rooted, listening to every word. She didn't want to interrupt. She would never have imagined this was how he'd made his money. His billions.

'My first success was everyone's. Because money came along with the tourists who wanted to stay in what I'd built. Social media influencers wanted a taste of civilisation in an uncivilised landscape…to take pretty pictures of sunsets burning over windswept olive trees. I brought tourists into the community that had once protected me. And I paid them back tenfold before I sold that little hub of opulence. And then I made it out. I got out of that village because of *me*. And with a little luck guiding the way I did it all again. All over Sicily. I took broken things and made them pretty. Sold them for far more than they were worth. It took me to Italia. To Roma. And there I built my business—Russo Renovations. And now my rebuilds are coveted. Worldwide.'

'Who taught you how to fix things? To build?'

'Myself. Books…' He hooked a brow. 'The internet.'

'And the London hotel?' she asked. 'Is that yours too?'

His eyes flashed and her stomach tugged.

'Mine,' he confirmed.

She nodded. It all made sense. Why he'd been there—why he'd been the one to find her. But it didn't sound as if luck had been the catalyst for his success, and she told him so.

'I don't believe it was luck that guided you,' she said.

He shrugged. 'What did, then?'

'Tenacity.'

'The boy I once was would have liked to hear himself called tenacious.'

'And the billionaire?'

'He wouldn't care.'

He smiled, but still it didn't reach his eyes. And she wanted to ask why he didn't care. But he'd already revealed so much. Told her a story so honest that she had goose bumps on her skin beneath her jumper.

'You asked me how I made my money,' he reminded her, stepping backwards so that his black-sheathed body was framed by the view of the sea. The vastness of it. 'Now I have told you. Are you ready?'

'I'm ready,' she told him—because she was. She'd lock away her feelings. Use the logical part of her brain to do what she needed to do. As she had been taught to do. *As he had.* 'I'm ready to take the pregnancy test now.'

Flora unbuckled herself and stepped out of the helicopter with an ease she didn't really feel. Because it wasn't about either of them, was it? This was all about a potential child.

Their child.

He moved to her and whispered, 'Welcome home, Flora.'

'Home?' she echoed. 'You live *here*?'

'*Si,*' he said.

She looked at his home. A floating kingdom of slick black and white lines and blue angles on a still ocean. With nothing but more ocean at its back.

She gasped, unable to hold it back. 'It's a palace!'

'Three hundred feet of space,' he confirmed

without ego. Without a smile. 'Multiple decks above and below sea level. Every toy at my disposal—every recreational device a billionaire could need. And twenty-plus staff to deliver everything on a silver platter.'

'A multi-billionaire,' she corrected, and smiled a smile she wasn't feeling. Because inside she was crying for the boy who had saved a village.

Because who had raised him?

His mother hadn't been able to look after him. His father had thrown him away, calling his illegitimacy shameful but doing nothing to fix it. Doing nothing to legitimise him. His father had hidden him away in a village where people relied on each other to survive.

The money…the opulence… None of it mattered, did it? But the story did. It was a story she'd like to tell her child. *If* she was pregnant. The story of how their father had lifted a village below the poverty line and turned himself into a billionaire.

The reality of it all caused her temples to throb.

The hand resting beside his thigh was so big, so strong. But all she could imagine was a smaller hand, a cold hand, attached to a hungry body…

She wanted to wrap her arms around his neck and pull him close to her, whisper words for the little boy she'd never met. She couldn't do that. But she could hold his hand.

She took it. Pushed her fingers through his and held the smile on her face in place as she said, 'Show me the way, Raffaele.'

'Flora…?'

Her eyes moved up the length of him. Over the muscular body of a man she'd never have guessed had once been hungry. Or cold.

'Raffaele…?'

'Why did you get off the chopper?' he asked.

'Because we want the same thing.'

His eyes narrowed. 'What's that?'

'For our baby—if I'm pregnant—to be protected. Safe.' She pulled in a deep breath and added, 'Loved.' And the last word caught her in the ribs.

Who was going to love her?

Who would love Raffaele?

Could she?

Raffaele didn't respond—because why would he damage the tentative connection they'd formed? The connection that had encouraged her to get her off the chopper? Why would he admit to her that he didn't love? That he didn't know how to love and didn't want to learn.

His mother had loved completely. With all of herself. *Selfishly.* She'd neglected everything around her because of that love. Until the promise—*the lie*—of its return to had driven her to death's door.

'What I told you has made you think that?' he asked.

He wouldn't have summarised his rise to wealth using those words. *Protected...safe... Loved.* He certainly hadn't been loved, protected, or kept safe.

'Yes,' she said. 'Your origin... Your beginning...' She shrugged. 'They're powerful.'

'They hold no power over me,' he dismissed. Because they didn't. He'd only told her because she'd asked. And the story he'd told her hadn't been his origin. It had been an ending. An end to the constant worry of watching over his mother. Because once he'd left that village he'd paid someone else to watch her for him.

Raffaele hardened himself against the woman holding his hand. The small wisp of a woman who'd broken his control, encouraged him with her whispers in the dark to throw that glass against the wall and let the shards fall where they might...

Step for step they moved along the deck. His hand absently pulled open the glass door and he led them inside. A sense of unease settled over him as he recognised the pull in his groin for what it was.

Desire.

His eyes raked over her. He wanted the softness of that hand holding his against his chest. He wanted to bury the memories she'd pulled out of his mouth in the warmth of her body. To find oblivion as he sheathed himself inside her and to drown out the part of the story he hadn't told her.

How could he tell her that the hand she held so softly, so carefully, hadn't been able to reach his mother? That he hadn't been able to protect her or make her feel safe?

His *mamma* had never grasped the hand he'd held out. Yes, she'd accepted his wealth. Accepted him turning that dilapidated house on the hill into a beacon of privilege. But she'd never accepted *him*.

So what did it matter that he hadn't been there? Would she have taken his hand that night when she'd seen no alternative?

He'd never know.

'Which way?'

Eyes bright, Flora turned to him.

'Raffaele?'

He swallowed down the lump in throat. 'Straight ahead.'

She smiled. A small, delicate pout of her lips. And, oh, how he wanted to lean down and sample their fullness. Taste her again. But this time

with his name on her lips. He wanted to hear
her panting it. Screaming every syllable into his
mouth.

Raffaele.

He tightened his hold on her hand and guided
her through the main saloon into the corridor
that broke off into multiple master suites. Led
her towards his suite. His room. His bed.

What was this woman doing to his control?

He'd enjoyed being anonymous. He'd enjoyed
her casual approach to his wealth. To him.

*Because you are weak around her and she
sees what you are. A lonely boy with a dream
of getting out.*

Had he ever really got out?

The fingers entwined in his flexed. He looked
down at the small hand. The elegant fingertips
pressing against his knuckles.

She didn't care, did she? About the wealth?
She'd asked him to take her to his bed, make love
to her, without even knowing his name. She'd
followed him across the sea. And only when his
yacht had been thrust in her face had she considered that he might be part of a world she wasn't.

He hardened. Every part of him throbbed with
an absurd need to be inside her. To drown in her
dismissal of his name and his wealth. Because
all that had mattered the night she'd met him
was what he was feeling right now.

An intoxicating need to be with her.

And he didn't understand it. This *need*. He didn't understand *her*. She'd cared about the *story*. The one he'd told no one. Her decision to get on his boat had come because of a story of weakness. Of *him* being weak.

He didn't even know why he'd told her.

Lies.

He knew. He'd wanted to make the innocent wonder in her eyes every time she looked at him vanish. To stop this hold she had over him. To stop this lack of control he felt near her.

But it hadn't stopped. It had intensified.

If you told her about your mother...how you failed—

He blocked the intrusive thoughts and focused on his next step. Their destination. Their fate.

He'd figure her out later. But first things first...

He pushed open the door to his suite and pulled her over the threshold without pause or hesitation. He was ready to confirm what he somehow already knew without rhyme or reason. She *was* pregnant. And in a few minutes he'd be bound to her for ever.

He wouldn't fail his own again.

That was his promise.

His vow.

He wouldn't look away this time.

CHAPTER SIX

RAFFAELE HADN'T SAID a word.

Every inch of his body was relaxed as he lounged on the cream leather high-back chair as if it were his *throne*, one leg lazily over the other, his arms languid. Hands that didn't tremble rested on the tips of the arms as the pregnancy test sat on the table between them.

Flora was not relaxed.

But his eyes kept her rooted. Perched on the end of the cream leather sofa, knees together, fingers steepled. *Waiting*.

He watched her, and she watched the pregnancy test.

Flora cleared her throat. It was too tight. Too dry.

She reached for the glass of water on the edge of the table. Far away from the device in the middle.

Tentatively, she raised it to her lips, careful to think through the steps. *Open her mouth. Take a sip. Close her mouth. Swallow. Put the glass back.* Rational steps. Logical.

The suite was all crisp lines in creams and greys. All shiny. The low table between them gleamed. If she leaned over—inspected the plastic blue and white oval device—she'd see her reflection in it.

They were in the bedroom of the master suite. *His* suite. Which was really as big as any house, with a separate dining area, a lounge and bathroom.

An enormous bed dominated one section of the room, with the crispest white sheets, the plumpest pillows and the deepest mattress she'd ever seen. Subtle lights surrounded it. Built into the walls themselves.

Only a soft glow, so as not to take away from the view, she assumed. Because the view of the ocean was vast, and it surrounded them. Neverending. Water usually calmed her. Her trips to the beach were her escape. Her chance to be still. To let her mind wander.

She couldn't look at it now. But she couldn't stop looking at the bed.

She flicked her gaze back to the test. It wasn't the kind of test she'd pictured in her head. It was smart. It wouldn't show her any pink lines. She wouldn't have to apply her maths skills. She wouldn't have to add one line with another to make two. *If* she was pregnant it would flash with the word *pregnant* and show how many weeks life had been growing inside her. She would know in less than five minutes what she hadn't known for weeks.

Unable to bear it any longer, she leant forward, reached out her hand.

'It's not time.'

Her hand froze in mid-air. 'How much longer?'

'Thirty seconds.'

She dropped her hand. Returned to her perch.

She'd asked Raffaele to read the instructions to her twice. It wasn't rocket science, but she'd wanted to make sure she did it right.

And, calmly, he had. Each word level. Clear. Emotionless. She'd known he wasn't telling her a story any more, but a part of her had wanted to hear what he was feeling. How he felt about her. About the possibility of a baby they'd made together.

Raffaele had whisked her through doors made of glass, through corridors that smelt of newness and quality, but when he'd opened the door to this room he'd let go of her hand. She rubbed at it now. There were no visible marks. No evidence of his touch. But she tingled with it. The sensation of skin against skin. All thoughts of the boy vanished and replaced with thoughts of the man beside her.

Of this room he'd led her to.

The bed.

She cleared her throat. Swiped her tongue against her teeth. That wasn't logical. She *needed* to be logical. Those feelings, those impulses that had gripped her when she'd walked in, that had urged her to climb onto the bed, to surrender to her body's needs, needed to be buried.

'It's time, *piccolina*.'

Her gaze snapped to his. Before she could stop herself, she spoke. 'I'm scared.'

'It can't hurt you.'

'What if I hurt *it*?'

He blinked. Slowly. Fluttering shadows kissing his chiselled cheekbones. 'Why would you think that?'

'No…' She stumbled, realising what that had sounded like. 'I wouldn't hurt a baby. I wouldn't hurt anyone. Not physically. Not emotionally. Not on purpose.'

Because that was always her goal, wasn't it? Not to hurt those she loved with her behaviour. Not to make them worry. But unconsciously…

'What if I get it all wrong?' she asked, her throat tight. 'What if I'm a terrible mother?'

His gaze softened. 'That you worry about

being bad means you will do everything you can to be good. That you will care. Deeply.'

She frowned. He'd told her his story… Didn't he deserve hers, too?

'Aren't you worried?' she asked. 'A little scared?'

'No.' His shoulders stiffened. 'I'm confident I'll know the things not to do.'

'How?'

'I wasn't always rich,' he reminded her, and she watched his Adam's apple drop and rise in the now open collar at his throat. The tie was gone. Laced over the arm of the chair. 'Our child will never have to worry about trading skills or finding the easiest route to a major city. I can provide all the things I never had.'

'Money doesn't equal happiness. Money doesn't mean love.' She shook her head, another long strand of hair breaking free of her loose bun. She reached up and pulled out the hair tie. Shook her head again until her hair fell about her shoulders. 'It's made of paper. *Things* don't raise a baby. People do.' She pushed the black band onto her wrist and turned her gaze to his. '*We* will.'

A pulse hammered in his cheek. 'Money will provide the foundations.' He unhooked his leg, planted his feet squarely on the cream rug beneath his feet. 'It will provide all the things we spoke about. Protection. Safety. Food. Central heating.'

'I was always warm...' An image of her mother and father flashed in her head, with their big smiles and open arms. 'Always safe.' She blinked away the unexpected tears obscuring her view. 'I never had to worry about the plumbing...the bills,' she continued, with a lump in her throat. 'If I was cold, my mum and my dad they turned up the heating. Hugged me. Wrapped me in a blanket. Tucked me into bed...' She whimpered and the dam broke.

He stood, but she held up an open palm.

'Please, don't touch me.'

He froze, eyes wide, and stared at her. 'Why not?'

'Because if you do—' she scrubbed the back of her hand across her eyes '—I'll cry.'

'You're already crying.'

She snorted. 'Oh, my God!' She pulled at the end of her jumper until it swallowed her hand and rubbed it across her offensive nose. How dared it make such a sound in front of—?

She looked up at the man watching her so intently. 'I don't usually make piggy sounds,' she promised, attempting a smile. But it felt too tight. Too pinched.

'It's not every day you take a pregnancy test.'

She looked at the test.

Her parents had claimed her. Wanted her. Always loved their adopted miracle baby.

No, they had always loved *her*, she realised. After London, after the file, there had only been one place she wanted to run to. Straight into the arms of her mum. Straight back home. Because that was where she'd always felt safe. Even though there were things her parents hadn't told her. Even though they'd sheltered her.

'Why are you so afraid when your childhood was a place of warmth?'

His question broke into the realisation it had taken her too long to understand. Her parents loved her.

'It's not just fear,' she admitted. She saw it then. The flicker of his shadowed jaw. The thud of apprehension. 'I'm not *just* afraid. I'm feeling a whole host of things I don't know what to do with.'

'You're allowed to feel everything,' he assured her. 'You can cry.' He winked. *'Snort.'*

This time, her smile was genuine.

'I burst into your life and turned it upside down. You will find your feet,' he promised, 'and I will help.'

'How can you guide me when you don't know the way, either? When you don't know me?'

'What do you think I need to know?'

'I…'

The room felt too small. Airless. He deserved the redacted parts of her story too, didn't he? The parts only she knew.

She dragged in a fortifying breath. 'How much of the report on me did you read?'

'The important bits.'

'Which were...?' she pressed. Because she needed to know what he already knew and the parts she'd have to tell him.

'Where to find you.'

'That's it?' She frowned. 'My address?'

He rolled his neck, as if the end of her tears had released his muscles. 'Can I sit?'

'What?' she asked, confused, and looked at the chair behind him. 'Of course. Sit down.'

'No.' He dipped his head to the space beside her. 'I want to sit next to you.'

'Oh...'

'Unless you don't want me to.'

She looked at the space between them. From his chair to where she was perched on the sofa. 'Okay...' A flush crawled up her throat. 'You *should* sit next to me,' she said—because he should. 'We should find out what the test says together, not while we're sitting six feet apart.'

He came to her. Soundless steps of solid muscle. Stalking towards her. He sat down. Mirrored her and perched at the end of the seat. He looked at the test, and she looked at him.

Her heart did a double beat. Now was the time, wasn't it? To give him all the facts. Before they looked at the test. Her story in exchange for his.

'Tell me what you know of my past,' she started, because it was the right thing to say. 'And I'll fill in the blanks.'

'I know that your birth name is Flora Campbell. You were born to a woman named Clara Campbell. Father unknown. Your parents adopted you at fourteen weeks old and you became Flora Bick.'

'Is that it? My file didn't tell you that my biological mother was an addict? That she was addicted to substances? Hard ones?' She swallowed, but didn't allow herself to look away from him. 'They were in my system when I was born. I was born an addict...' Her chest hurt and she rubbed at it.

His fingers flexed on his knees and, absurdly, she wanted to hold them. His hand. Not for him this time. But for herself.

He turned his body, his gaze, and she locked on to the warmth of him. The reality.

'You can tell me.'

He needed the facts too, didn't he?

She pushed out a silent breath 'I have an addictive personality.'

'I know. You said so that night.'

Had she?

She felt as if she'd said so much and yet so little. She swallowed the urge to relive every moment of their time together. Every word. Every caress of his fingers. Every kiss.

'I obsess. And I'm impulsive.'

'Your impulsivity brought you to me,' he countered. 'To my bed.'

He didn't touch her, but his words shot straight to her stomach. They arrowed with piercing accuracy to the feminine heart of her. She pulsed with the memory.

'What if I give the bad bits to the baby? The things inside me? What if I can't—?' She struggled to find the words she needed to explain.

'We might have made a baby, *piccolina*. How can a baby be bad?'

'My parents have always encouraged me to stay in control of my emotions. To be led by my head and not my heart—to measure my impulses against what the consequences might be. I didn't do that in London. I just wanted—' she sucked in a lungful of air '—you.'

'Our attraction isn't something to be viewed as toxic. It's natural, Flora. It is human to desire. To want. You acted freely in London. You were driven by your feelings and you expressed them without remorse. Without restraint. How can it be a bad thing to be free?'

'Free?' she echoed.

Something strange was happening in her chest. It was getting lighter. The burden of expectation she'd carried around her whole life was being lifted.

'What if you do not let fear of what you can't control overtake this moment? What if you pick up the pregnancy test and see what it says? Be present in this moment and nowhere else?'

His eyes held hers and she clung to them. To the anchor of them that was holding her steady when she felt rudderless.

'I understand your fear—' he said.

'How?' she interrupted. 'How can you understand?'

'Because I understand the fear of the parts inside us that we can't control,' he said, his jaw determined. 'The things that live inside us that we cannot change. My mother was depressed. Deeply so. I didn't realise it was a condition until my teens. I didn't understand it was a mental illness. I only understood that she was very angry.' His nostrils flared. 'With me.'

He dismissed the platitude she was about to use.

'I'm sharing information that you think is important,' he said. 'Your biological mother was a drug addict. Mine was very sick. You think your mother's sickness might live in you, that it reveals itself in your impulsivity. If you believe

that, then my mother's illness could live in me
too. The difference between what came before
and what comes after is the choice we make.
The knowledge we use to guide us to make the
right decisions.'

'Is that why you told me you would marry me
before we even knew we needed options?' She
swallowed, trying to organise everything that
had happened in the last few hours. 'Because
you—?'

'Because I need to know that what is mine is
safe. I will keep you safe,' he promised. 'Both
of you.'

Her breath hitched. She believed him. He was
claiming her—*them*—even before they knew if
the test was positive.

'I'm still scared, Raffaele.'

'No. You're not afraid of this.' His eyes flicked
to the test. 'The baby does not scare you.'

'What do you mean?'

'You're scared of the night you let your guard
down…leaned in to the woman *inside* you…'

He placed a hand on his chest, fingers splayed,
and she wanted to touch them. Place her hand
on top of his.

'Because the woman you let out,' he continued, 'upheaved your world. Shook it to its roots.'

'She upheaved your world too,' she added, reminding him that she wasn't the only casualty of her actions the night they'd met. 'Not just mine.'

'No. We did it together,' he corrected. 'We claimed that night, and now we must claim this moment too. Know who we must become to raise a child. *That* is what scares you, *piccolina*, isn't it?'

'What…?' she asked.

But he was so close to putting all the facts she'd given him together. So close to seeing the part of herself she hadn't revealed, had been too afraid to voice.

'Who you are with me.'

She felt…what? Relief? No, it was more than that. Her skin prickled. Her mind itched. She wanted to close the inches between them on the sofa and thank him. For seeing what she couldn't.

She closed her eyes. For just a moment she shut him out—and the test, the future—and looked inside at herself. Saw the fear of breaking the rules and hurting those around her, and the worry of who she might become if they didn't rein her in…control her impulsivity and her need to have what she wanted.

Her eyelids snapped open. She had wanted him, and together they might have made a baby. And he was right—how could that be bad?

'Be brave,' he said. 'Choose to be yourself. For you...for our baby.'

Her breath caught. 'You are so sure I am pregnant, Raffaele?'

The darkness of his pupils panned out. Spread to turn his eyes into a pulsing ring of colour. 'As sure as you know my name.'

'Have you always been so...*sure*? Of everything?'

'Always.' He swallowed thickly. 'I've always known what it is I must do. Who I must be.'

'And you just...do it?'

'Yes.'

Could it be so simple?

Flora wanted to be brave. She wanted to be herself *for* herself in every moment. In this one and the next. She liked the woman she'd been in London, and she liked the woman sitting next to him on the sofa now.

Raw and honest. That was what they'd been with each other since they'd met. Physically in London. Emotionally in the middle of the sea. And he hadn't flinched. Hadn't looked away from the person she had presented to him. He was *encouraging* her to be herself.

She leant forward, reached out and took the test in both hands. She glanced up at him. He wasn't smiling. Wasn't hurrying her to turn the test over. He was waiting. Because he knew what it would say and so did she.

She turned it over. 'I'm pregnant.'

It wasn't tears this time, as she'd expected. And it wasn't fear making every hair on her body stand to attention. There was a quiet joy in her chest. In her heart. She handed him the test but he didn't reach to take it. He looked at her as she looked at him.

They locked on to each other's eyes.

Looked at each other.

'*We're* pregnant,' she corrected, and couldn't help the smile.

'So we are,' he agreed. His voice was low. Deep.

The bomb had detonated and yet the shards weren't piercing her skin. She was not collateral damage. She felt determined. Empowered. Safe to explore what she was feeling. And she was feeling everything. And the man beside her was giving her time to feel. Explore those feelings. Define them.

His stillness was a weighted blanket. His confidence soothed her…and it all came to her in a flood. The need to protect her child. To raise it with love and hope. The way her parents had raised her.

The Bicks. It made sense now, their over-protectiveness. They'd done it all because they loved her. Because they'd claimed her as theirs and she *was* theirs. She was Flora Bick, the daughter of farmers. And she loved her parents. Did they get everything right? No. But they did it all from a place of love. For her. Their daughter. The kind of love she already felt so deeply—so quickly— for the baby in her belly.

Her baby.

'I need to call my mother.'

He nodded and reached into his inside pocket.

'Call your mother, *piccolina*.'

He handed her the phone, and with trembling fingers, she took it.

'What happens next?'

He shook his head. 'No.'

'No, what?' And then he did what she hadn't expected. What she hadn't seen coming. He touched her. With both his hands. He cupped her face, held it steady, and looked at her. *Really* looked. And she felt seen. With all her flaws on display. And still he held her.

Raffaele thrust his fingers deeper into her hair. 'Be present,' he told her. 'In *this* moment. Not the next. Talk to your family.' His fingers pressed into her neck. 'Then *we* will talk.'

And she wanted them to. Because they needed to figure out what came next. What they wanted to come next. What she wanted to come next.

Did she want to focus on the baby? The baby's needs for the future? Or did she want this moment to be about *them*? Future parents. Once lovers. They were bound now by the biggest secret of all. They were going to become an unexpected family…

Only one way to find out…

She leaned in until she felt the heat of his breath on her mouth. One more inch and her lips would meet his. A tremble raked through her. She closed her eyes…

He shifted, feathering his lips against her forehead. And then, before she could analyse what that type of kiss meant, he was standing.

She met his eyes. Tried to figure out what she saw there.

'Call your family. Tell them that you are safe, you are warm, and you are pregnant with my child,' he said, and held her gaze for a moment too long. It steadied the hands that still trembled. 'But tell them you won't be coming home.'

She nodded. And he was gone. Striding out through the door and closing it behind him without a sound.

Flora kicked off her pumps, pulled her legs up beneath her and crossed them. She placed the pregnancy test beside her, in Raffaele's vacated seat. Then swiped up on his phone and punched in the numbers for home.

Flora talked to her mum. She asked her not

to speak. She told her she loved her. Loved both her parents. And she told her she was about to become a mother herself. And that she hoped she'd be able to love her baby just as much as they loved her.

She told her that she was safe, but she wouldn't be home for a while, because she had to get ready for parenthood with the father of her child.

She was going to marry Raffaele Russo.

Flora Bick would be his wife.

Because she *was* Flora Bick—daughter of dairy farmers.

She always had been.

Her mother sobbed. Said words of love mixed with a little fear and a lot of joy. And Flora ended the call with her mother's excited voice still in her ear.

It was time to stop ignoring her needs, wasn't it? Because they were natural, weren't they? Natural to her, anyway. Instinctive.

She pulled her jumper over her head and threw it onto the sofa, along with Raffaele's phone.

Flora was going to listen to her instincts. She was going to twist those fancy taps and fill that claw-footed bath with bubbles and climb inside it.

Because, right now, she wanted a bubble bath.

CHAPTER SEVEN

RAFFAELE OUTSTRETCHED HIS arms and placed them flat on the veneered surface of the long, rectangular table. Two place settings and enough food to feed fourteen people, hidden beneath silver cloches, waited for them on a table that had never seen so much food.

Sitting in his glass cage of opulence, he'd never felt more exposed. Every wall looked out to the sea apart from the one leading from the bedroom. Where she was.

He scrubbed a hand over his chest. His chest was on fire. The idea of eating—

He swallowed down the thought.

She would eat and he'd watch.

He pinched his lips together. He hadn't needed the pregnancy test to confirm he'd been right to chase her.

His baby was growing inside her right now.

Picking up a glass, he swallowed down ice-cold water. Felt it travel down his throat. Into his gut. But it didn't ease the burn. The rawness of the last few hours was making his stomach twist and tug.

He'd exposed more of himself to Flora than he ever had to anyone. He'd dug deep into memories he'd buried beneath his billions and spoken of them as if they didn't matter and had little consequence to his life. He'd exposed his weakest self.

And instead of demanding she go with him—instead of picking her up and throwing her over his shoulder to his bedroom to take the test, to get proof that their one night had had consequences—he'd told her his story. And she'd been seduced by the truth. Had given him her truth in exchange.

Why had he done it? Talked? Why had he given his story to her? The facts. Unvarnished.

Because he hadn't been able to stop himself.

But he hadn't expected to see himself mirrored in her words.

In her honest vulnerability.

The confession of her fears had given voice to words he'd never had before. He'd never spoken aloud of the things that lived inside him. He'd pushed them down deep. Ignored the possibility of them and their destruction. His mother's mental illness... His father's ability to destroy...

reject…abandon. He was made from weakness too, and they'd formed a connection.

Connection? His face twisted in displeasure. It was chemistry, not a *connection*. And that part didn't matter. Only the baby. Only keeping Flora healthy.

A host for your heir?

He rolled his shoulders. A host for his heir sounded cold. Emotionless. She was not cold. She *felt* things. Made *him* feel things.

The burn in his chest was setting fire to his throat.

He must be sick…coming down with something. The flu?

He pressed an open palm to his forehead. He didn't have a fever.

What was wrong with him?

There was a rap at the door.

He sighed. Heavily. More food.

'Entra!' he called absently, and picked a piece of invisible lint off his cuff.

'Raffaele…'

His eyes shot to the door and there she stood. The slight wisp of a woman who'd infiltrated his life and turned it upside down. And she was wet. Her hair was dark, almost black, hanging limply over her shoulders.

'Flora…' He said her name and, oh, it tasted

sweet to his tongue. Eased his indigestion... calmed the roughness of his throat.

A rush of yearning pulsed through him in waves. To get closer to their baby. To get closer to *her*. To inhale her clean scent and comb his fingers through her hair.

'Why did you knock?' he asked, focusing on anything but the scent of soap clinging to the air and seeping into his lungs.

'Because it's polite. I'll always knock if the door's closed. But if it's open...' Her eyes flashed with challenge. 'I'll come inside.'

She moved into the room. Her movement drew his gaze to her bare feet, to the knot of her ankle bone, where an angry line ran across her otherwise perfect skin. He wanted to kiss the imperfection. Bring it to his lips.

He concentrated on her legs. The taut, milky skin of her calves, leading upwards to where the hem of his white shirt kissed her thighs.

She stopped at his side. The delicate warmth of her body hit him. She raised her arm and held out his phone. His eyes shot to her fingers, to the elegant digits. He reached for it. His fingers brushed overs hers. Connection zapped through him. *Chemistry.*

She stepped back. Disengaging their hands. She felt it too. *Still.*

He looked up at her, standing above him, looking down at him. Soap and warmth seeped through his nostrils. Delicate scents that he couldn't place, but that he recognised were only hers.

He would recognise her scent anywhere. The subtlety of it. It punched him in the gut, that sense of knowing. Of familiarity.

'Open doors are not always an invitation to enter, *piccolina*.'

The black of her pupils washed through the brown. 'But sometimes the temptation is too hard to resist…'

He felt it. The shift. The pulsing between them of the shared memory of that night six weeks ago when she'd entered his domain uninvited.

Her mouth parted. She exhaled. He wanted to taste her. Her mouth. Her lips.

He should have kissed her. Pushed his lips against hers when she'd invited him to do so. Should have celebrated the confirmation that she was pregnant in the same way all this had started. With his undiminished need to be inside her.

Why didn't you?

It wasn't the time.

Lies. You're afraid of who you are with her.

He was not afraid. He was in control. Of all things.

'You're to be the mother of my child. You do not need to knock,' he said throatily, and swallowed down the lust storming through him. Making his blood heavy. Hot. *'You,'* he said, reinforcing his words with unrelenting arousal thickening his voice, 'will enter whichever room you like, take any seat you want. You need no one's permission.'

'Not even yours?' she asked.

'Not even mine,' he answered. Too quickly. Too easily.

It roared through him then. The temptation to stand, to push his chair back and hold her by the hips. Place her on the veneered table. Step between her thighs, between the legs that he knew would fall apart for him on command. Push the plates covered with silver cloches onto the floor and sink inside her. Untether the leash of rigid control as he had six weeks ago. To pop every button on the shirt that she wore and reveal the nakedness beneath with his teeth.

And she *was* naked, wasn't she? Under his shirt? He could see the pink shadows around her puckered nipples pressing against the silk. The swell of her breasts…

He hardened, painfully, and tried to turn off the image in his head of a naked Flora in his arms. Beneath him. Moaning…

Now was not the time for kissing, either. Not when his control was hanging only by a thread.

Raffaele cleared his throat. Looked away and

purposely broke the spell. He placed his phone on the table next to his empty plate. 'Would you like something to eat?' he asked, and lifted a cloche to reveal some chocolate-covered delights.

'I'd like something else to wear.'

He placed the cloche back over the food and trained his gaze on the next platter of food. He wouldn't think of his shirt next to her skin. He would not think of a naked Flora in his bath. Drying her body with his towels. Leaving her scent all over his bedroom, as she had in London. He'd still been able to smell her scent there only hours ago. Now here she was, in the flesh. Spreading her scent everywhere.

'You don't like my shirt?'

He lifted another cloche. *Porridge?*

She wrinkled her nose and lifted her arms. The sleeves hid her hands. 'It's a little big.'

He replaced the cloche. 'Clothes are arriving for you within the next thirty minutes.'

'You have clothes arriving?' She pointed a hidden finger at her chest. It looked like a handless arm. 'For me?'

'You are the one stealing my clothes in the absence of yours.'

'Borrowing,' she corrected.

'Sit. Eat.' He squared his shoulders. 'The clothes will come.'

Dear God, he hoped it would be soon, or his erection would never go down.

'A laptop and a mobile phone, too.'

'You didn't have to do that, but thank you.' She sat in the white leather seat next to him at the head of the table. Her eyes moved over it. 'Do you always eat so formally?'

'This can hardly be called a formal meal. You're wearing a shirt and nothing else.' His eyes moved over her—the open collar at her throat, the buttons undone just enough for him to see the subtle swell of her breasts.

'It's a *white* shirt.' A blush warmed her cheeks. 'They're always for best, aren't they?'

He cocked a brow. 'Sunday best?'

'It's Tuesday.'

She laughed. A gentle titter of breath. And there was the burn again in his chest.

'But something like that.' She reached for another lid and lifted it. 'Pancakes? Did you have someone cook the entire breakfast menu?'

He had.

'You didn't eat breakfast.' He looked at his watch. He should have ordered lunch. Even an early dinner. He frowned. 'Give me a list of the meals you would like and a menu will be prepared.'

Eyes wide, she interrupted. 'For my preference?'

'*Si*—who else's?'

'Yours *and* mine, maybe,' she answered, and used a pair of tongs to scoop several pancakes onto her plate. She lifted another lid and found fruit. She spilled a heaped ladle-full on to her plate. 'In our house it's eat it or starve.'

'Eat it or starve?' he repeated. 'I'm not familiar with the phrase.'

'What there is to eat, is what there is to eat—so you eat it.'

'But you live on a farm.'

'A dairy farm.' She rolled up the sleeves, revealing her delicate forearms. 'So there's always milk.' She picked up her cutlery and paused. 'Are you eating?'

'No.' He bowed his head towards her plate. 'But, please…'

Knife and fork in hand, she looked at her food. 'Aren't you going to ask me how it went?'

'I can see how it went,' he said. 'You've had a bath.'

'A long one,' she agreed. 'But that's not what I meant.'

'I have no desire to know what happened on the phone with your family,' he dismissed. 'The only family I care about is sitting at this table.'

That stung.

'*I* care,' she whispered.

His gaze narrowed. 'So I should?'

She heard the inflection of his words. The question.

Quietly, she put her cutlery down and gave him her full attention. 'They're my family. Of course they should matter.'

'To me?' he asked. 'Why would they matter to me?'

A boy with dark hair curling around his ears appeared in her mind without invitation. A boy dipping torn bread into cheese and handing it to the shadow of a woman she couldn't picture. Couldn't conjure anything but that shadow, which appeared as clear in her mind as a photograph.

'Don't you understand?' she asked.

But how *could* he understand? Her family wasn't perfect, but...

His gaze flicked to the left and then zeroed back on her within the flash of a millisecond. 'Understand what?'

Flora's heart stopped as she took in the deep frown lines between the darkly shaped eyebrows, the focused intensity of his gaze.

'They're your family now, too.'

Slowly he nodded, and she let out a breath she hadn't realised she was holding.

His hands flexed where he'd placed them on the table. 'What do they need?'

'What do you mean?'

He splayed his fingers, palms forward. 'Is the farm in some sort of financial trouble?'

'Of course not,' she dismissed. 'The farm is doing well. The farm is fine. What does that have to do with anything?'

'Their livelihood—your family home—is safe?' He frowned. 'Then they don't need *me*.'

'Parents are not accepting dowries these days, Raffaele, and I'm pretty sure it used to be the other way around.'

'Dowries?' His frown deepened, before vanishing completely. Leaving his face a smooth mix of understanding and relief. 'How much would they like?'

She shook her head. 'No, that's not what I meant.'

'Then what *did* you mean?'

Flora shifted in her seat. Twisted her bottom and joined her knees until she faced him fully. 'No payment is required. No membership fees. We are having a baby together, so our families will…' she held her hands out in front of her and pulled them far apart '…merge.' She clapped her hands together.

The frown returned, and her urge was to stand up and place her thumb at the base of those lines. Swipe upwards and smooth them free. But she didn't. She sat and waited for him to join the dots. For him to understand what she meant.

They were all family now, whether or not he understood it.

'You will take *my* name,' he intoned.

'They'll still be my family. And my mother's birthday is in two weeks.'

'We will be in Sicily,' he interjected.

'Sicily?' she asked. 'I thought you lived here? On the boat?'

'We can't raise our baby on a super-yacht.'

'You want to raise the baby in Italy?'

'Sicily,' he corrected. 'I want to raise *our* baby in Sicily.'

'Where you grew up?'

'Yes.'

'Why? I thought you said it was out of the way? Won't we need a hospital?'

'The village is not what it once was.'

'Because you changed it?'

He nodded. 'We will have no trouble with transportation. Nor with access to a hospital. Most things will come to us. And they are already being organised.'

'Like what?'

'A doctor.'

'A *doctor*?'

'To make sure your pregnancy is going as expected.'

'Why wouldn't it?'

'You can ask the doctor. It is just a formality. Something to tick off the list.'

'You have a list?'

'Several.'

'Can I see them?'

'They are in my head.'

'Download them for me and we can compare notes.'

'Unfortunately my brain isn't connected to the internet.'

'Summarise the lists for me,' she said, 'and then we won't have to figure out how to connect you.'

'We will get you some clothes first. Then travel to Sicily, where we will be married—'

'Married?'

'By next week,' he answered, as if this was the most normal thing in the world. He looked out of the window at the greying clouds. 'If the weather holds, even sooner.'

'Why so fast?'

'Why not?' he asked nonchalantly. 'And after the wedding we'll prepare the house for the birth of our child.'

'The house you grew up in?'

'The very same.'

'I'd like to see where you grew up, and my parents would like to meet you.'

'Impossible,' he dismissed.

'Why impossible?' she asked, when no explanation was forthcoming.

'My pilot has taken the chopper to collect clothes from a boutique in Cornwall.' He named the shop.

Flora gasped. 'They dress celebrities!'

'Now they dress billionaires' fiancées too,' he added smoothly, and her heart hiccupped.

'I'm not your fiancée yet.'

'Semantics,' he dismissed. 'When my pilot returns,' Raffaele continued, 'we lift anchor,' he said. 'We will arrive in Sicily in three days—a week at worst.'

'Okay…' She placed her hands on her thighs, squared her shoulders and put on her most serious face. 'First, you need to *ask* if I'd like to marry you—rather than *tell* me I will. Second, *if* I agree to marry you, you need to ask if I'd *like* to take your name.'

'Would you like me to get down on one knee too?'

Her stomach flipped. He was good on his knees… A blush heated her all the way up from her chest, to turn her cheeks into a crimson beacon. She ignored it. And her wayward thoughts. And the memory of his kisses.

'The words will do just fine,' she said.

His chest puffed out. 'Flora?'

She swallowed thickly. 'Yes, Raffaele.'

'Will you marry me and take my name?'

'Is that one question or two?'

Thick eyebrows arched. 'Pardon?'

'Will I marry you is one question, right?'

He dipped his head. *'Si.'*

'If I say yes to marriage, but no to taking your name, does that instantly cancel out the first question, so the second doesn't really matter?'

He was trying to take control of her life, and she wasn't sure if she was grateful or overwhelmed. Both, she realised.

'Flora.'

The sound of command in her name stopped her mid-sentence.

'Why are you avoiding the question?'

She pointed her toes and rose on the balls of her feet. 'Which one?' she asked. Because maybe she wasn't ready to give her thoughts voice. To part the rational ones from the illogical. 'Marrying you or taking your name?'

'There's only one question—which you understand perfectly.'

'I do,' she admitted.

'But you're not ready to answer it?'

She already knew the answer, didn't she? Hadn't she already decided?

She had, but she'd only accepted the *idea* of marriage. Now he was actually asking. Now he was making the possibility a reality.

And she didn't want the answer to be decided for her. She wanted to be an active participant in her own life. Not just pulled along on someone else's schedule—someone else's plan for her.

'Do I really have a choice?' she said. 'Or did you ask simply because I requested that you did? If I hadn't brought it up, would you have simply lifted anchor and sailed away to Sicily?'

'Yes. I would have.'

She folded her hands across her midriff and looked at her untouched plate. *Honesty.* She appreciated that. But—

'If I don't give you an answer now,' she asked, and reached for her fork, moved it beside her knife, 'what will you do?'

'I will wait.'

Her eyes snapped to his. 'Until you get the answer you want?'

'Until you give me the answer that is yours and yours alone.'

Hers and hers alone? She sucked in a deep lungful of air and held it in her chest until it burned. 'What if you have to wait for ever?'

'For ever is a long time,' he said. 'But I'm asking for for ever.'

He shrugged in a gesture of indifference. Because he knew she'd give the answer he wanted and this was just a play for time?

'It only seems fair you ask for the same from

me,' he finished, and her heart squeezed. 'But I do not understand your hesitation about marri—'

'My hesitation has everything to do with my life before *this*. Before *you*. Because then I didn't have choices. I just acted. I don't want to just act. Take the next inevitable step,' she corrected. 'I want to be an active participant in my life. In my decisions.'

'Explain it to me,' he urged. 'Tell me about how your life has been.'

'My parents always encouraged me to do the right thing. To be logical—rational. In control. To ignore my feelings and embrace structure. If I was ever in doubt, I followed the path of routine. Other people's plans for my life.'

'And you chose to do this why?'

'It was all I ever knew. And following someone else's plan was always easier because it made my parents happy. I was home-schooled… sheltered…'

'Sheltered?'

'From anything that might have…' Flora hesitated.

'Introduced you to something that could sway your tendencies towards addiction?'

'Exactly. But I didn't know that. So I did everything they requested of me. I ignored my tendencies to obsess. I tried to be the kind of daughter I thought they wanted—'

'And forgot what *you* wanted?'

Her shoulders sagged. 'Exactly.'

'What kind of daughter did they want you to be?'

'They wanted me to be safe. I understand that now. Since I found out about the adoption. My biological mother...'

'They wanted to keep you safe from yourself?'

She nodded.

'But if you weren't allowed to explore your natural personality, how could your parents—or you—know you were a risk to yourself?'

'They didn't. Couldn't. But they did it because they love me.'

His chiselled jaw hardened into angles of determination. 'If marriage wasn't an option, what would be your choice? Would you want to be a single mother? Raise our child alone? Put it up for adoption—?'

'Adoption?'

She thought of the lonely boy with a mother who didn't care. She thought of her biological mother, who had given her up.

She hoped her birth mother had done it out of a kind of love, in the hope that she would find a family like the Bicks. That her daughter would be raised with love and hope as an anchor in this world. She had been lucky to have found her parents. Because the root of her childhood, and all her teenage years into adulthood, had been a constant love. Family.

No, they hadn't got it all right, but she would work through those feelings later, with her mum and dad. All that was important to her right now was their love. And she had that. In abundance. And she wanted that for her baby. Their unexpected family.

'Adoption would never be a choice for me,' she said.

'I am presenting you with what the other options would be if you chose not—'

'I don't want any of those options.'

'Then what *do* you want?'

'I…'

Raffaele thrust back his chair, closed the distance between them, and before she could fully dispel the breath in her lungs he was on his knees before her.

'I'm listening,' he told her. 'I'm not afraid of you, and you shouldn't be afraid of yourself. Afraid to give voice to the thoughts in your head.'

'What's happening in *your* head?' she asked, because she wanted to know. Wanted to know him better.

'I want to know the answer to a different question,' he asked.

'Ask it.'

'Why were you in London?'

'To collect my adoption file from the local authority. I'd found out six months before that my parents weren't biologically related to me. I fell—'

'And broke your ankle?'

'How do you know that? From your investigator?'

'The scar.'

His head dipped to her feet and he claimed her right foot with his palm. His thumb stroked against the ugly pink scar running the span of her right ankle above the knot of the bone.

'How did it happen?' he asked, keeping his head bent, continuing the rhythmic stroking of her scar, back and forth. Back and forth.

She trembled. 'I didn't listen to my head.'

'What did you listen to?'

'Instinct...' she breathed. 'There was a storm. It moved some slats on the barn roof. They just needed to be pushed over. Back into place.'

'And you wanted to fix it?'

'I wanted to fix it,' she agreed.

He placed her foot back onto the cold wooden floor and placed his hands on the armrests either side of her. She didn't feel trapped. She felt *cocooned*. Cushioned from the world and its expectations of her. In a bubble where she could be free, surrounded by the strength, the power, of his presence.

'I fell,' she confessed. 'My ankle…it was badly broken. And it was as if everything my mum and dad had feared happened in an instant. It only took one choice—one bad choice—to follow my urges and it ended badly. It ended *very* badly, Raffaele.'

He didn't push. He sat back on his heels and waited for her to tell her story, to give him her version of events in her own words.

'My parents had always known the circumstances of my birth—the drugs in my system. It was in my medical records, too. The doctor at the hospital explained that I should be careful with the strong painkillers that he wanted to prescribe to me because of my history with addiction. That's when my parents confessed that I was adopted. After that I did everything I could to find out how to locate my birth parents.'

'And you ended up in London?'

'Six months later,' she confirmed. 'To collect my adoption file from the local authority. And it said so much and yet so little.'

He frowned. 'Why were you wearing a ball gown?'

'I saw it and tried it on. I liked how it felt against my skin. I'd never had anything like that.

And for once I didn't want to stop myself from doing something that I wanted to do.'

'And the hotel? Few farmer's daughters visit The Priato.'

'I wanted to step out of my life—just for a night—and experience things I never had. So I booked myself in and—'

'Found me just when your world was imploding?'

'Yes,' she said huskily.

'And now it is imploding again you want to take a minute? Work through your emotions before you make a rational decision?'

He understood her. He understood why she couldn't accept his proposal right now, even though she wanted to.

Raffaele leaned into her, his height meaning they were face to face, with her sitting down and him on his knees. Eye to eye.

'What are your instincts telling you to do?'

'To marry you,' she answered honestly—because she'd already decided. But she had to understand *why* she'd made that decision. Was it impulse? Or was it logical? Did it have to be either?

'Trust them,' he said. 'Your instincts.'

'What if it's the wrong decision?'

'What if it isn't?' he countered.

Her heart thumped in her chest, because her

real fear was that she was going to fall so completely into this man's eyes she wouldn't be able to see a way out. And how would he guide her when he didn't know she was falling?

A question hit her. Announced itself loudly in her brain. So she asked it. 'Why were *you* in London?'

His mouth compressed and his hands slid away from the armrests. He stood. 'You know why.'

'Because you were grieving.'

His eyes hardened, but she pushed because she wanted to know. To understand him. *His* choices.

'But why London? Why that—?'

There was a knock at the door.

Flora jumped to her feet like a startled teenager and crashed straight into his chest. She looked up into his face, her palms resting on hard muscle. She could feel his heart beneath her fingers. A heavy thud which matched her own.

Simultaneously, they both looked at the door, and before she could ask him not to answer it, but to answer her question instead, he strode towards the door and yanked it open.

After a few minutes of whispered murmurs in Italian with whoever was on the other side of the door, he turned to her.

'They're lifting the anchor in fifteen minutes,' he informed her, and his eyes told her this was it.

She must decide.

Was she in or out?

Flora stared back at him, at this beautiful man she'd made a baby with, and squared her shoulders.

She'd thrown her doubts and her needs into the world and someone had listened—*he'd* listened. He had got down on his knees and talked her through her feelings. Without judgement. Without pressure.

However flighty she'd been, he'd listened to her needs—not told her to ignore her emotions, but to work through the choices that were available and come to a logical conclusion. She hadn't had to choose her feelings over rationality. She'd combined the two. They'd worked through her feelings. Her thoughts. *Together.*

She was in, wasn't she? *All in.*

The thoughts and the lists in his head that she wasn't privy to pushed at the corners of her mind, but she held them back and focused on him, on this moment, and staked her claim.

'I'm ready,' she declared—because she was.

She stepped towards him. Put one foot in front of the other and felt her stomach fizz with an unknown feeling.

Anticipation?

No. It was excitement.

His bulk covered the entrance to the door, but as she approached he stepped aside and there was a woman. Smiling at her.

'Grace will show you to your room,' he said, nodding towards the smiling stranger.

Flora didn't smile back. Her eyes snapped to Raffaele's and her excitement fizzled out into a frown. 'My room?' she echoed.

'The VIP suite,' he answered, without a flicker of hesitation.

'And where will you sleep?'

'In my bed.'

Without me?

The words hugged the inside of her vocal cords. They were going to have different rooms. Separate beds. New rules for their life.

Realisation dawned over why he'd refused her mouth—*her kiss*—earlier.

He didn't want her.

Raffaele just wanted the baby.

CHAPTER EIGHT

CONTROL.

For the last four days he'd been trying to cling on to it, and every day it miraculously came to him. Because it had to. Because she was here, and she was carrying his baby. She was safe in his palace on the sea. He would feed her, dress her, listen to her. But he would not take her to his bed.

He wouldn't lose control again in the delicate contours of her skin. Would not kiss the freckles on the bridge of her nose as he counted eyelashes so long he didn't understand their growth.

He couldn't keep her safe if he did that, could he? If he allowed himself to get too deep, to feel too much?

But every day her eyes begged. Moved over him at breakfast, at lunch, at dinner. With agonising *want* in her eyes.

And by God, he wanted too. Pulsed with it as he answered questions about his hotels, his renovations, his ability to strip things apart and put them back together. About how the deconstruction of something whole could reveal its secrets.

The Priato—his hotel in London—had many such secrets. Not only the secret door she'd found, but tunnels and concealed rooms. She'd asked if he would take her back there, to the place they'd met, and reveal them to her. Expose the secrets the previous owner had concealed from all but a select few.

She'd asked for more details about his business, about Russo Renovations' global allure. And he'd answered. He'd nodded or shaken his head when she'd asked about his family. No, she couldn't meet them. He had none. No cousins, no aunts—just him.

It had always just been him. On the outside looking in. The generosity of the community had given him a bowl or two of freshly made pasta covered in home-made passata to take home, but no one had ever invited him to sit at their table.

She'd told him stories of her life as she sat beside him on the sofa, a blanket pulled up to her chin. She'd left her feet exposed, dangling her toes over the edge, wiggling them. Cute little digits he'd longed to reach for. To apply pressure to the ball of her foot. Massage the flesh.

He hadn't touched her feet. He had not touched *her*. But he had listened. And that was new to him. Because he never listened. Not to the women he took to bed. Not to the women who hung on his arm, adorned in the glittering diamonds and jewels he presented them with before he shooed them away. Bored when his sexual appetite had diminished.

It was not diminished for her.

His hunger for her had intensified.

But he'd made himself pay attention to Flora's words and not her body. Because he'd wanted to hear them. Her words. Her voice. And she liked to talk…to ask questions.

She'd told him of her life on the farm. Of cousins. Of aunts and uncles. Growing up with a family. Birthdays, Christmases, holidays together as a family.

His family now. Supposedly. Because of the child growing inside her.

The sky rumbled. His already white knuckles clenched harder around the metal rail. He looked up and let the rain, which had only been a drizzle moments ago, beat down on his face and closed his eyes.

He prayed for control now.

'Sir?'

The boat rocked, but he did not loosen his grip. He turned to his captain, his jaw set, and readied himself.

His captain's eyes were wide and unblinking, and he said, 'We still can't find her, sir.'

A roar bloomed inside him. Puffing out his chest. 'Three hundred feet of space and you can't find her? You navigate across the sea,' he said, his chest burning, his voice hoarse. 'Multiple decks above and below sea level are under your control. Every technological device is at your disposal to locate land, some off the map. You have twenty staff below you in rank to support you. And yet—' he swallowed down the fury in his throat '—you cannot locate one woman?'

The captain held out his umbrella for Raffaele. He pushed it away, let the elements which were accelerating in speed punish his body.

Because he deserved to be punished, didn't he?

He'd lost her.

Misplaced a whole woman.

'She's still aboard the ship.'

'You know this?' he countered. The wind carried his voice to create a formidable growl. 'You can report this as a fact?'

'Anchor dropped less than an hour ago.'

'And not everyone is accounted for,' he interjected cuttingly.

He ran tense fingers through his hair. Sliding the wet strands backwards.

'The storm will pass,' his captain assured him. 'Everything is in place to ride it out. A boat of this size is more than equipped to deal with any storm, sir.'

Raffaele gritted his teeth. He understood his captain's intentions, and he knew what his boat was capable of. It would withstand extreme weather. This was his home, and he spent half his life at sea. His boat was safe.

But he knew the backlash of storms. The tragedy. The last one—

He slammed the door on that memory.

It was a different kind of storm today.

His boat was a cut above all other superyachts, with its cables creating a lightning shield from masthead to bow. The glass bridge held various devices and instruments worth hundreds of thousands of dollars to warn them of incoming weather via satellite. There were radars to see through a storm. Closed circuit television triggered by radio announcements and alarms recorded strategic points on the boat.

'Have you checked the CCTV footage?' Raffaele asked, and clenched his fists to try and stunt the urge to grab this man by his shirt and rattle him until he gave the answer he wanted. *Needed.*

'Of course.' His captain shook his head. 'Nothing. No sign of her. But there's so many places to hide. So many rooms to explore.' He dragged in a stuttering breath, and promised, 'We will find her.'

Drops of water ran over Raffaele's forehead,

down his haughty nose, and dripped onto the soaked decking. Absently, he dashed them away.

'She will be found,' he agreed stonily. 'But not by you.' He moved unseeingly past him and called over his shoulder, 'Go back to your bridge, *Captain*,' he sneered. 'And keep your staff indoors. Look after your responsibilities.' He tugged open the door to the lounge. 'I will take care of mine.'

His heart clenched. Refusing to beat. Refusing to let him move until he acknowledged the words he'd refused to hear. To consider in his conscious thinking because of it what they meant.

He'd failed. Again.

Because they were *all* his responsibility. The staff. The crew.

It wasn't his captain's fault that a freak tropical storm had headed straight for them as they sat idle in the middle of the Mediterranean Sea—a storm expected to peak in two days' time.

It wasn't his fault that the storm had dragged all the staff and occupants of the super-yacht from their beds before the sun had graced them with its unsuccessful efforts to clear the sky.

Raffaele looked at the waves. They were like a foaming, galloping herd of angry stallions.

He shoved back the sleeve of his sodden jumper.

It was nearly six.

But what was time when it seemed his had run out?

Another rumble shook the boat. Shook him from the outside in with a startling clarity.

It was Raffaele's responsibility to make sure every member of his staff was safe. Protected.

It was Raffaele's job to account for every unforeseen danger. To guard against it. To protect his own.

It wasn't the captain's fault Flora had not been in her bed when a head-count had been made. She should have been in *his* bed. Next to him… under him. He didn't care what position.

Only that she was *safe*.

And she wasn't.

Lightning flashed and every glass window, every polished surface, reflected the ferocity of the storm that had headed their way. He moved inside through the double doors, felt the wind pushing them closed behind him.

Raffaele just stood there. Taking in the reinforced double port windows. His boat was a 'go anywhere' explorer super-yacht. The biggest of its kind. The safest.

She had to be here.

He'd found her once. He would find her again.

Toes. Ten of them. Perfectly formed and unadorned. They peeped out from beneath a heavy red blanket with golden edges—the perfect camouflage. The sofa she was sprawled out on was an exact match. Of all the nooks and crannies, the multiple rooms, the suites, she'd chosen to come here.

The Sky Lounge.

The rain beat down on the glass roof. *Pitter-patter. Pitter-patter.* His ears whooshed. His skin tingled.

He didn't know if he'd been standing there for minutes or hours—only that he'd found her.

He'd ascended the spiralling stairs and there she'd been. His legs wooden, he'd moved soundlessly across the carpeted floor. No lights were lit. There was only the low light from the darkened sky above them. The chandeliers glinted in the shadows like strands of suspended diamonds.

He stood in front of her sleeping figure. She was huddled deeply beneath the heavy blanket in the furthest corner. Hidden out of sight. All but her feet, which were dangling over the edge of a gold-leaf-decorated sofa with mahogany trim. Oblivious to the storm. Oblivious to him.

He closed his eyes. Let it sink in. The subtle scent of her. The presence of her crawled over his skin. His body. Was it relief her felt? It didn't feel like relief. He couldn't breathe. His lungs wouldn't inflate. His mind wouldn't stop—

'Raffaele...?' Flora spoke his name in a soft caress.

His eyes snapped open. Zeroed in on her sleep-flushed face. His heart crashed against his ribcage.

Her warm brown eyes shone with surprise. The blanket slid down her bare shoulder as she sat up and brought her legs in front of her. She wore nothing but a blue silk vest and matching shorts.

Every emotion he'd been holding in check, every feeling he hadn't given a name, pulsed to the surface of his skin. His face contorted. Rage burnt through him. And he homed in on that anger, the swell of it inside him, and spat its heat into existence.

'Don't you *ever* do that to me again.'

'Do what?' Flora asked huskily, the grogginess of sleep lifting as though she'd never closed her eyes.

She stood, the blanket pooling around her feet. She stepped out of it. Inched towards him. Never had she seen his features so drawn. So tight.

Her eyes moved over him. The body-fitting black jumper clung to every muscle of his chest, revealing hardened abs. His dark blue jeans—

She inhaled deeply, and trembled.

He was soaked through. He looked like a man who had battled the kraken and won, but somehow, she realised as her gaze moved over his face, had also lost. There were no visible bruises, no wounds, but haunted eyes met hers.

Her hand moved of its own volition to his cheek. 'What's happened?'

He shrugged her off and she felt it like a physical blow to her sternum. The veins in his neck bulged.

'Raffaele?'

The heavens opened above them. Rain hammered down on the glass roof. A rumbling roar of thunder filled the electric silence.

His nostrils flared.

'The storm?' she asked, eyebrows high on her forehead.

'I couldn't find you,' he said, his jaw tight, his mouth barely parted.

'I couldn't sleep...' she replied, her brain buzzing.

'So you climbed to the highest room?' he asked, his voice low. Grim. 'Went to the darkest corner and hid beneath a blanket?'

She half turned to the sofa and splayed out her hands at her temporary bed. 'I wasn't hiding.'

She turned back to him, her chest heaving, her feet planted firmly to the floor, and readied herself for a fight she did not know how to win because she didn't understand the stakes.

'I fell asleep listening to the rain,' she explained, and made herself breathe. Slowly. Deeply through her nose. 'Why are you so angry?'

'I am not angry.' He moved to her, a half-step which brought her face directly in line with his chest. 'I am *furious*,' he hissed between gritted teeth.

She lifted her chin defiantly. 'You said I could go through any door—take any seat—'

'Not in the middle of a storm!'

She stilled. Eyes turning wide. Those tight muscles… The rasp of his breath… Her eyes ran over him again.

'You're…' she pressed her open palms to his chest '…you're trembling.' Instantly she pulled her hands away and looked down at the wetness coating her fingers. 'You need to take this off.'

Her hands travelled to find the hem of his jumper and—

His fingers, a steel band around her wrist, halted her attempt to lift the wet wool away from his skin.

'What happened?' she repeated her earlier question.

'*You* happened, *piccolina*.'

'What do you mean?' she asked, her brain doing somersaults to try and make it make sense. 'Have I done something wrong?'

Quick as the lightning flashing above them, he released his hold on her. Stepped back.

'Why are you so afraid?' she whispered, her heart pounding.

'I'm not afraid.'

She heard it. The lie. He was terrified.

'You have no reason to be angry with me, Raffaele. Or furious,' she whispered. Quietly. As if trying not to poke at whatever beast he was containing inside the hunch of his powerful shoulders.

'What is it?' she asked again. 'What's turned you into such…'

'A mess?' he finished for her roughly. His Adam's apple was moving heavily up and down the length of his taut throat.

'I wouldn't choose those words,' she rejected. 'You don't look a *mess*. You're…' She reached up and stroked her hands along the rigid lines of his shoulders. 'You're a barely contained mass of energy.'

But she wasn't scared of his power…of his barely contained emotion. She dropped her hands to her sides. This wasn't anger. She could sense it in the heavy air surrounding them.

Her brows knitted. 'It's not the storm you're afraid of, is it, Raffaele?' Her insides twisted. Her brain flashed with every conversation they'd had since leaving the farm. 'Were you afraid for me?'

Her mouth ran dry. Goosebumps rose all over her skin. She felt exposed. Naked. She ran her fingers over her arms and folded them across her chest. *She* had scared him.

Flora retreated into her head. Into her body. Back to the place she always went when she got it wrong…hurt those she loved.

Loved?

She swallowed down the pain in her throat. Looked at the man watching her every movement with such intensity she felt it. *Inside.*

How could she even consider that what she felt might be love when he didn't want her?

He wanted the baby.

He didn't even want to take her to bed.

She pressed her fingers into her arms to centre herself. She'd thought they had a connection. Talking over breakfast, dinner, lunch…

'Why? I thought—' She'd thought she understood the rules, but this wasn't the game she'd thought she was playing. Not this game of…of *fear.* 'I thought we were becoming friends. Finding some sort of common ground—a companionship. Of sorts…' She sniffed. 'Some kind of a foundation for marriage as we won't be having sex—'

A growl interrupted her. A deep, wordless roar of denial. She ignored it. Ignored him.

'You couldn't find me,' she continued. 'And you were afraid of where I might be—what choices I'd made during the storm. You were *concerned,*' she sneered, but it bit at her, the hotness of tears.

Flora refused to let them turn her into an emotional wreck. She wouldn't revert to doing the right thing. *Saying* the right thing.

'You thought I was going to do what? Stand outside with a metal stick and wait for lightning to strike? You thought I might compromise my safety—the baby's?'

He reached for her. 'Flora—'

'Don't you dare tell me I'm wrong.' She stepped back until the backs of her legs touched the sofa.

'You *are* wrong.'

She pointed a trembling finger at the centre of his chest. 'Don't you dare contradict yourself. Your boat is an explorer—you told me—and it's built for extreme weather. Because this is your home— where you come back to after every renovation… every job. It's safe because you made it to be safe. Built it—designed it,' she corrected breathlessly.

'Nothing is completely storm-proof,' he explained, but she shook her head.

'You feared for me, Raffaele,' she said.

Old hurts bloomed fast. The barn—the fall— her night in London. Was everybody right not to trust her?

'How can we get married?' she asked.

'You're pregnant—'

'Yes. I'm pregnant. But how can I marry you when you don't trust me?'

CHAPTER NINE

'It's not you,' he confessed. 'It's the—'

Every instinct told Raffaele to hold his tongue. Not to speak out loud. Not to bring back to life the memory he'd buried deep, so very long ago.

He knew why he was overreacting. Knew why he'd put all his regressed pain into her and turned it into something ugly. *Angry.*

And then she'd pushed against his rage. It had replaced his rage with guilt. Regret. He'd hurt her. And the only way he could fix this…

He didn't want to remember—didn't want to share it with Flora. But it pushed at the edges of his mind…pushed itself inside. Uninvited. The memory of being lost—misplaced in plain sight.

No one had noticed for three days. No one had reported him missing. Raised the alarm. No one had checked in on his mother…

Words wouldn't come.

He couldn't speak.

'How could you think I'd put myself in danger?' she asked.

'No, I didn't.' He rejected her assertion and curled his fingers into his palms to resist pulling her into him. Holding her shivering body against him to infuse her with any warmth he had left in his skin…give it to her.

His friend? His companion? His lover?

He squashed the thoughts down. He didn't need friends. He couldn't allow her to be his lover. And he didn't deserve companionship. But she'd offered all of them freely since her arrival. Talking about the future. About the past. *Her* past. Full of love and devotion for her family.

Now *his* family.

People he hadn't met—didn't want to meet.

So what had he done? He'd squashed all those hopeful words from Flora's mouth under his big foot because of his past. His neglectful family. His mother.

No. This isn't about your mother. It's about you.

A gush of air escaped his mouth.

It *was* about him. His overreaction was rooted in the roots of his existence. Because he had been born from neglect. To a mother who should have been keeping an eye on him. But who never looked his way. Never looked at him when it mattered. And then he'd done the same. Looked away at the wrong moment. Neglected his responsibilities.

'I thought *I* had put you in danger,' he confessed. His chest heaved. 'Do you understand? I couldn't find you…'

Her arms flew back around her midriff and he wanted to prise them open and climb inside her embrace. Press their bodies together in an intimate, unbreakable lock.

What was wrong with him?

He was a mess.

A frantic mess.

'But I wasn't lost, Raffaele.'

'You were lost to *me*,' he growled. 'It's protocol, in any extreme weather, to do a head-count of all the staff and residents on the boat—'

'I didn't know that,' she interrupted. 'I didn't know a little bit of heavy rain would be of concern to a boat of this magnitude. I wanted a different space—a different view.' She looked up at the glass roof.

'This is only the beginning,' he told her. 'A storm like this will only get worse. Reach a peak we won't fully understand until it arrives. I've seen—'

'I didn't know that either.'

'It was my responsibility to tell you, *piccolina*.'

'I'm not your responsibility, Raffaele.'

'You are carrying my child,' he reminded her. 'I should be protecting you. You should be in my bed, where I can see you, keep you safe.'

'*You* chose separate bedrooms. *You* chose—'

'To stay in control.'

'You chose not to be with me in a physical sense even when you said it was natural.'

'It *is* natural.'

'Then why—?'

He couldn't help it. Raffaele reached for her. Held her elbows in his big palms as if she were the last point of safety. The only lifeboat when he was sinking deep into uncharted territory.

'Have you not enjoyed my company? Have I not been enough to keep you entertained without sex?'

He had to know. Had to know if, despite what they'd shared, all she wanted was the billionaire. The façade. The man who offered women nothing but sex.

'Of course I've enjoyed it. The last four days have been heady. Real. Honest.'

Real? Honest? Those two words punched him in his temples. Rocked his stance. Weakened his knees.

They had been real. He'd never spent so much time with a woman. Never eaten three square meals with another human being every day.

Meals without the due ceremony of a restaurant, a chef, a menu.

Never had he eaten a meal on his lap with some flickering film in the background as a woman showed him how clever her new laptop was.

Never had he refused to take a willing woman to bed.

Never had he listened to a woman speak.

Of course he'd heard the phonetic hum of her words, but he'd never wanted to understand what they meant. How words spoken revealed truths about the speaker. *About Flora.* He'd wanted all her words. To stay in an idle stupor and pay attention to her chorus.

Had he been a fool for wanting that?

'Couples do more than share the same bed. Couples have disagreements, they worry, they fight,' he said, before he could pull the words back.

He smoothed a hand across his forehead, but knew the deep frown lines grew deeper.

She didn't blink at his choice of word. She counter-attacked without hesitation. 'Couples trust each other,' she corrected. 'My mother and father—'

'This has nothing to do with your parents. It is about us navigating our way to a wedding. Marriage. The birth of our child.'

'You say you haven't had a long-term relationship. Neither have I. But my parents… Of course they quarrel about the small things—and the big things. But they trust each other. Support each other. They don't chase each other across one hundred acres of field just because one gets up early and goes off somewhere on the farm. They don't think the other one is in danger because it rains and they can't see them.'

Her freckled nose wrinkled.

'Because at the end of the day,' she continued, 'my parents sleep in the same bed.'

He heard the tremble in her words. He wanted to press his mouth to her, steady that tremble. Swallow the pain he'd inflicted and put it back where it belonged. Inside him. *Contained.*

'That's a couple,' she said. 'They're a couple. I don't know what we are—what we can be when you've let everything I told you about my past turn you into a wild man searching for a person who wasn't lost just because it was raining.'

'It's a storm.'

He tugged her closer until she was pushed against his chest. The warmth rocked him to the core. The instant flare of need.

Mine.

The word roared through every vein. Every brain synapse.

Safe.

That word hummed in its wake.

He dipped his head lower. 'Not once did your past cross my mind when I couldn't find you,' he said, his voice gruff. 'Not once did I think of the stories you've shared with me since I came into your life on the farm. Not once did I worry about what your parents fear—what *you* fear—about your past.'

And he hadn't. His worry had been purely selfish. Driven by his need to know that she was safe, that she was protected.

She arched her neck defiantly to meet his gaze dead-on. *'Liar...'*

The whisper of her breath teased at his lips. Hardening him. *Everywhere.*

'Why would I lie?' he growled.

'Why *wouldn't* you?' She flicked the pink tip of her tongue over her lips. 'You want this marriage because of the baby. And you need me to gain both. But you don't *want* me.'

He knew he had made her believe that. It had helped him stay in control. But now he had to be honest. With himself...with her.

'I want marriage,' he agreed. 'I want our baby, too.'

Their gazes clashed. Locked. Hers was a sad glare of triumph. His pulsed with a need to tell the truth. So he did.

'But I have never stopped wanting you.'

His confession was a low growl of truth. Of honesty. They'd spent the last four days connecting like normal people. Acting like a couple.

'You want me?' she repeated, slicing through his internal justification of what was happening to him. To *them*.

'And what do *you* want, *piccolina*?'

'Does it matter?' Her eyes flashed fire. 'You don't trust me.'

Attraction. *Desire*. It simmered beneath the surface. His unwavering need to be inside her. But she deserved the truth. A truth he could no longer deny. A truth he would not deny her any longer—because she was right.

'I don't trust *myself*.'

He thrust the truth into the air pulsing between them, and she caught it.

Her eyes widened. 'Tell me why?' she urged, and his heart thudded with his mistakes.

It all came out in a flood. 'I was trapped in a storm once—by a fallen tree. I couldn't get home for three days. I was stuck. Too far from the house, too far from the village to call for help.'

'What about your mother? Didn't she come looking for you?'

He shook his head.

Brown eyes narrowed below arched brows. 'How old were you?'

'Eleven…twelve…' he answered absently, his

chest heavy with the memory. 'I'd had to walk through a pathless tree line to get to the next village. We needed things, and no one in my village had any odd jobs for me. It started with drizzle. Then came the thunder. The winds...'

'What happened?'

'I fell, and so did a tree.'

'And it trapped you? The tree?'

'For three days.'

'Were you hurt?'

'It wasn't broken bones I was worried about. And it wasn't the hunger. Not even the rain.'

'What was it?' she asked huskily.

'I couldn't get back to—'

'To your mum?' she asked.

'I was found three days later. By Matteo the village bar-owner. There was devastation *everywhere*. The tree...it saved me. Sheltered me when no one knew I was missing. I had no broken bones...was only suffering from exposure. Shock. Bruises. But my mother—'

He tried to hold it at bay. The visceral memory that was flooding his every sense.

'When I was carried back to my mother she was in a stupor. She hadn't eaten. We both went to the hospital that day. Airlifted. I will never forgive myself for many things, but not making it home in that storm—I couldn't look after her.'

Horror filled her eyes. 'You could have *died*, Raffaele.'

'And so could my mother. One day later—even an hour later...'

'No, *you* could be dead.'

'I am alive,' he corrected.

And the biggest punch in the gut was the memory that came next. A memory he wasn't ready to share. *Couldn't* share. Because then she would know that the storm hadn't been the only time he'd failed his mother. Failed to be there for her when she needed him.

And the next time had been fatal.

A tear rolled down her cheek and he closed his eyes. Shut out the pity he did not deserve.

Her fingers feathered his jaw. Gentle. Soft. He released her elbows. Pushed away her tenderness.

'Look at me, Raffaele...' she breathed. 'Open your eyes.'

He did, and met the innocence of hers. The pity.

'You can't control the weather. You're not responsible for storms. You weren't then and you're not now. Do you understand?'

He couldn't speak. Wouldn't lie. It *had* been his fault. Then. And after...

She grabbed his hand and placed it on her chest. The thud of her heart pulsed against his palm.

'I'm safe,' she said, and then she pulled his hand down between the centre of her breasts and pushed the flat of his palm firmly but gently against her stomach. 'And so is the baby.'

'Piccolina...'

'I'm listening,' she said.

She was smiling at the endearment he'd used on this night when her size had been small against the mass of him, but her presence had been mighty and all-consuming. And now she stood before him again, touching him. And hers was the biggest presence he'd ever felt.

She was bigger than the storm.

Louder than his desire.

She deserved the truth, didn't she? The truth of why he hadn't taken her to his bed? Hadn't been there to weather the storm with her?

'These last four days...' he started, refusing to let himself hold back. She deserved this much. She was to be the mother of his baby. She was to be his wife. 'I've held you at bay. Said goodnight and watched you close the door with me on the other side. Because—'

'Because?' she prompted gently, and her small hand was still on top of his, both sheltering the baby inside her.

Their baby.

'The night we met I was out of control. I allowed myself to lose control. And when you disappeared in London, with the possibility of my baby growing inside you, I promised myself I'd never let myself feel that way again. But you make me feel—'

'Out of control?' she finished for him.

He swallowed thickly. 'Completely.'

'You're afraid of who you are with me?'

'I'm frightened of the man I could become in your arms. That I will forget my duty—my responsibilities—that I won't be able to protect you.'

'Then we will protect each other.' She moved, gripping his face and standing on tiptoe. 'We can keep each other safe in the storm, Raffaele,' she said. 'And we can control *this*.' She leaned in and feathered her lips against his unmoving ones. 'This is natural. This desire. You told me so. So show me you're not afraid of me—because I'm not afraid of you. And you shouldn't be afraid of yourself. Be with me the way I want to be with you. Let's choose to be the people we are with each other and let's make this work. Prove our marriage can work because we *choose* it. We choose *us*.'

It snapped. The leash on his control. And he thrust his mouth on hers. Pushed his fingers into her hair.

Raffaele had claimed his choice.

He pushed his tongue into her mouth. She

gripped onto his shoulders, thrust her hips against the hardness of him.

'I want you so badly,' he confessed into her mouth. 'I desperately need to be inside you, *piccolina*. I hurt. The want… It hurts.'

She broke free from his embrace, just enough to reach down to the hem of his jumper. He lifted his arms instinctively and let her pull it off.

He trembled.

Desire flared in her eyes. She looked from his mouth to his chest and discarded the jumper at their feet. She placed her hand on his chest. 'Trust me to make it better,' she said, and he thickened—his blood, his erection. 'Trust your body to tell you what it needs…because I need you.'

She reached for the hem of her silk vest. The blue silk had darkened from the wetness he'd transferred from himself to her. The fabric stuck to the outline of her breasts, her peaked nipples. She pulled the vest over her head.

'I want you,' she said. 'And I trust this is the right choice. So trust me to navigate the next steps.'

He growled, gripping her wrists and pulling her bare chest to his. He'd asked for her trust using exactly the same words…could he do it?

He wanted her. Her words. Her softness.

He chose this. Chose to trust in the moment's truth. In the realness of it.

Even if it was just for now.

Until the storm passed.

His kiss was urgent, demanding. And she gave herself up to his possession. Surrendered to the passion, they'd been denying themselves for four whole days and four long nights.

Flora was breathless. An urgency pulsed through her to feel more than his hard chest against the heavy swell of her breasts, or the push of his muscles against her peaked nipples, or the swell of his shoulders under the bite of her fingertips.

She wanted it all.

Trembling fingers reached for his belt. He stilled against her, but she wouldn't deny herself what they both clearly wanted. She wouldn't let doubt about who she was make her refuse to voice her needs. Because she trusted them. Her needs. And he trusted them. And now he needed to trust her. Trust himself to be the man he was with her.

Because she wanted this—the person he'd been for the past four days and the man who was shuddering against her.

She wanted this moment.

For ever.

She'd fallen straight into his eyes, hadn't she? But she didn't want to find the way out. She wanted to fall deeper. She'd fallen in love with this gentle giant who wanted to keep her safe. Protect her. Marry her.

She was in love, and love guided her hand to unbuckle him. And with her whole heart, with all that she was, all she was allowing herself to be at this moment, she knew fear would not beat her away from life again in case she hurt those she loved.

She was a woman who would claim the wants of her body and the needs of her heart from this day forth.

Because what was life without risk? Without choice?

It was a tick list. Safe. Predictable. All the things she no longer wanted. She wanted choice, and she wanted risk. Because she felt safe to explore the boundaries with this man now beside her…didn't she?

'I need you inside me, Raffaele,' she pleaded breathlessly. Euphorically.

She demanded what she wanted. What she needed. And he didn't deny her.

His hand beneath her bottom, he picked her up. He didn't speak. He backed her up, step by step, as he deepened his kiss, until her back met the wall.

The storm howled above them. Mirroring the howl of her body. 'Love me, Raffaele. Trust yourself to love me. *Now*,' she demanded.

And he moaned into her mouth and she swallowed the sound. The *power* he was giving to her.

With one hand still holding her bottom, he reached for his jeans, dragged them down over his backside until his erection pressed against the heart of her.

She moaned, and he broke free from her mouth, both of them panting.

'Say it again, *piccolina*. Tell me you need me inside you,' he rasped, his chest heaving. 'Tell me,' he urged, his eyes intense, looking at nothing but *her*. 'Tell me you need me.'

'I need you inside me, Raffaele…' She sucked in a shallow gasp of air as she said the words she wanted to say and the words he needed to hear. 'I need you.'

He reached down to the barrier between them and with a roar ripped her underwear from her body. He claimed her mouth. Closed his eyes and thrust inside her.

She tore her mouth from his and screamed his name. *'Raffaele!'*

She clung to him, panted her ecstasy into existence as he loved her body with a ferocious intensity.

This was living.

This was life.

This was love.

Flora grabbed his face. 'Look at me,' she demanded. 'Open your eyes and see me.'

Still moving inside her, he opened his eyes. Saw her.

And she saw him.

'I trust you,' she declared. 'Let go.'

His jaw tensed.

'Trust yourself.'

The pulse in his cheek throbbed frantically. 'I...'

She felt him holding back. Holding on to the fear. So by instinct she tilted her hips, taking him deeper into the pulsing, clenching heart of her.

'Come for me now, Raffaele,' she demanded. 'Let go.'

He thrust harder, deeper inside her.

'Yes,' she whispered. *'Yes!'*

Harder, deeper, faster, he thrust. His eyes never leaving hers until the moment had nowhere to ascend to. Only the greater pleasure of climax.

'Flora!' He gripped her hips, roared his release into the world, into her, and let go.

And so did she. Clinging to the man she was in love with. The father of her baby. The man she was going to marry.

Raffaele buried his mouth in the crook of her neck. She smoothed her fingers through his damp hair and panted in sync with his every breath. Their booming hearts pressed against each other in a crushing caress.

Flora placed her lips to his forehead, inhaled the heat of him, the vulnerability of this moment. But she wasn't ready to tell him. Confess her love. Not in the throes of ecstasy. Not in the storm that had set his mind and body on edge.

He raised his head, his breathing shallow and deep. He rasped, 'That shouldn't have happened.'

'You're still inside me,' she whispered.

And she couldn't help it. Her muscles contracted around him as if to prove her point.

He groaned deep in his throat, the skin pulling tight across his cheekbones. 'It shouldn't have been like this.'

'What should it have been like?' she asked, her voice just as low as his. But she didn't let the rejection in his words penetrate her mind. Because she recognised it for what it was.

Fear.

She'd lived with it her entire life—had felt it when he'd confronted her and thought she was missing.

He feathered his fingers over her hips. 'I came to you in anger…a *misplaced* anger,' he corrected. 'I never should have put my reactions because of the past on you. I see that now.'

'But I did the same thing,' she said—because she had, hadn't she? 'Your fears smashed against mine and exploded into—'

'Sex.'

The hands at her hips pressed into her hipbones and lifted her, breaking their intimate seal and bringing her to her feet. He tugged up his jeans and then reached for the blanket on the floor.

He wrapped it around her shoulders, cocooning her nakedness. Concealing it. But the rawness remained and she wanted to explore it. To explore her feelings. To make him explore his.

But he'd retreated. Physically. He'd stepped back until the distance between them was a palpable length. And emotionally she felt it too. As if the words they'd whispered between kisses had never been spoken. As if he hadn't released whatever power the storm had over him into her body.

'And wasn't that reaction normal?' she asked. 'The sex?'

'It shouldn't have been so desperate. So animalistic.'

'But it was. Because that's how we were feeling.'

'It shouldn't have been like that for *you*.'

'Why not for me?' She swallowed thickly. 'I wanted this. I wanted you. And you wanted me too.'

'You are *pregnant*,' he interjected fiercely. 'And I…' He exhaled a shaky breath. 'I took you against a wall…without softness, without care. I could have hurt you…the baby—'

'You didn't hurt me. Pregnancy doesn't make me breakable.'

'How do you know that?'

'I was raised on a farm.'

'We are not animals, Flora.' He scrubbed a hand over his face. 'We are human beings.'

She let her breath calm and tried to clear her mind. It wasn't the pleasure he'd given her that had pushed words of love into her head, was it? It was him, filling her mind, her body, her heart…

He kept on ripping apart the doubts she presented to him…the fear that who she was wouldn't be wanted. Because he wanted her. Despite his best intentions to stem the urgency in him to—

Love her?

She searched his face. Ran her gaze over every tight muscle. Heard the shallow rasps of his breath. Even if he was feeling things for her he wasn't ready.

And you are?

She was ready because she refused to be anything else. Refused to hide from her feelings any more. But him? He was a man who had loved her body in his grief six weeks ago—a man now vulnerable and raw from the memory of a storm that should have killed him who had loved her body today.

If she could persuade him to explore this side of their relationship, maybe he'd…

'We're going to be stuck on this boat for a few more days, aren't we?' she said.

'Yes.'

'Until we leave, I want to do everything we've been doing. Sharing breakfast…all our meals. And at night I want to explore this chemistry between us.'

'Burn it out?'

'Understand it,' she corrected. 'Give it a place in our lives before we get married. Before we have a baby. So you don't fear it.'

'I am not scared of sex.'

'But you *are* afraid of having sex with me. Why?' she asked, eyes narrowed. 'Because of the intensity of it?'

His eyes darkened. 'Because I can't protect you when I'm buried deep inside you.'

'I don't need protection.' She clutched the blanket closer around her midriff. 'I need—'

'Not this,' he said roughly. 'You need—'

'I need you to stop sweeping our attraction for

each other under the carpet. I'm tired of hiding from the elephant in the room,' she interrupted honestly. 'But if your goal in our relationship is to keep me safe…what better way to protect me than keeping me close? Isn't that what you said? That if I'd been in your bed then you could have protected me from the storm?'

'Flora…' he growled.

'Let's go to bed, Raffaele. Give this side of our relationship enough time to either run its course or…'

'Or?'

'Or we accept our chemistry as part of our lives.'

His eyes intense, he prowled towards her. 'The things I could teach you, *piccolina*…'

Her eyes travelled down from his thick throat to his broad muscular shoulders, then to the fine black hair over his washboard abs, and lingered on the V leading down beneath his jeans.

His muscles rippled with tension. Her insides clenched with instant desire. To be with him. *Again.*

'Then teach me, Raffaele,' she said, and her heart hammered.

Because she knew—could feel it in the heart of her soul—that the boy who'd become a man, whose mother hadn't loved him enough, whose father had rejected him, didn't understand family and didn't know love.

But she did.

'You want me to teach you the pleasures of the body?' he asked.

'Yes.'

He reached for her, put his thumb and forefinger beneath her chin. He gripped it, looked into her eyes. Searched them. Deeply. And she let him seek out her secrets, let him understand what she wanted, with her unflinching stare.

His voice ragged, he said, 'Until it burns out?'

'*If* it burns out,' she insisted.

'It will,' he assured her.

'And you want that?'

He moved his hand down her chin to grip her throat with light fingers. 'I want the self-control not to touch you.'

'Love me until you can control yourself, then.' Her mouth parted and she lifted her chin and pushed it into his palm. 'Until you can touch me without feeling the way I feel when you touch me.'

'*How* do you feel when I touch you?'

'I want you,' she admitted. 'Inside me. Again and again.'

He swiped his thumb against the hammering pulse in her throat. 'And now?'

'I want to make love all over again,' she said.

'The temptation to do it again doesn't frighten you any more?' he asked. 'That feeling made you run from my bed once…'

'That was six weeks ago. I'm not that woman now. I'm not afraid.'

'You should be.'

'Not of you,' she replied without hesitation. 'And not of myself,' she said.

And those words felt powerful. *She* felt powerful. Fearless.

She let the blanket slip from her shoulders. 'Not of this…'

He moved his hands to grip her hips and drag her body into his. 'Just until we leave the boat,' he said, his mouth hovering over hers.

'Or not,' she replied, and moved forward to catch his mouth.

But he leaned away. 'It will end,' he promised, and then he slammed his mouth against hers. Making his words the last.

Flora thrust her hands into his hair and pushed her tongue into his mouth. She was going to make sure his promise was one he couldn't keep. He might teach her the pleasures of the body. But she would teach him love.

Teach him to trust it.

To trust her the way she trusted him…

CHAPTER TEN

THE STORM HAD PASSED.

Raffaele slipped the grey button through the hole that housed it. Then the next. Methodically. Without emotion. He reached his throat and pushed the last button through the loop. He picked up his tie from beside the basin. Threaded the charcoal silk through the collar of his matching shirt. Flipped and twisted it between his fingers and pulled, forming a knot against his neck.

He reached for his suit jacket, pushed his arms through, and only then did he meet his reflection. Stare at the man who had stepped on this boat seven days ago and, regardless of what had happened in between, would be leaving as him too.

The man in the suit.

The billionaire.

In control.

Resolute in his decision, he turned. His leather shoes slapped against the marble floor. The burn in his chest set fire to his throat. He knew it wasn't indigestion. It was the burn of the man he'd been for the last three days, disgusted at what he was about to do.

He was going to take back control of himself. Of all their lives. His. Flora's. The baby's.

This piece of paper with its numbered lines would end whatever step out of time he'd allowed himself these past three days.

He picked it up from the gilded table, opened the bathroom door and stepped into the master suite. The bedroom.

And stood there.

Looking at the evidence of how the last few days had overturned his life.

Flora.

She was everywhere.

The white towelling robe he'd draped around her after their swim, only to discard it as soon as they'd closed the door to their rooms, flung on the back of a chair.

Her black panties lay on the floor. Panties he'd slowly taken down her thighs on the sofa last night. Gently teasing them down her legs and over her ankles to present himself between her legs on his knees and taste her.

The taste had lingered in his mouth and drugged him into a stupor of desire. He hadn't been able to sate it. That desire. That need to grip her hips, lower her onto any available surface and thrust himself inside her. Again and again.

In the pool.

On the floor.

The sofa.

The bed.

Slowly, he let his gaze fall on every piece of evidence of her until his gaze came to Flora herself. Asleep. Oblivious. A white sheet drawn up to her hips, her bare back exposed, her brown hair spread out over the pillow as her hand rested on his side of the bed. His vacated spot.

He'd left.

And he wasn't going back.

He couldn't. Not the man who had draped his arms around her, pulled her to his chest in the Sky Lounge with a blanket shared between them as they watched the storm.

Because she'd been right. He had needed to give this part of their relationship a place in their lives. And now he had. And it would remain on his boat. The intensity. The chaos.

In the real world, he wasn't the man who had claimed her softness with his unrelenting urgency. Nor the man who had accepted her tenderness, her cuddles, her laughter.

His heart hiccupped painfully in his chest.

He couldn't let himself be weak. He couldn't

let emotion in. On the boat, it had been simple. Keep her close—keep her safe. But in the eastern hills of Scarlata, in the house on the hill, he would need all his senses. A rational mind.

Raffaele squared his shoulders. It couldn't be helped. She'd refused to talk about what would happen next. When they got to Sicily. To the house that had never been a home. A house they would turn into a home now. To wipe away the past.

Why? For redemption?

Stepping further into the room, Raffaele shook the question off. The decision to go back had nothing to do with redemption and everything about giving his child roots, didn't it?

He sat down on the edge of the bed and feathered his fingers down her bare spine. He'd kissed each dip. Memorised it with his tongue. Tasted it with his mouth. She tasted of rain and sunshine. And the taste made his guts twist like a never-ending storm inside him.

That morning in the Sky Lounge he'd allowed the instant rush of desire flowing through his veins to gather in his loins. He'd lost his head. Given in to the temptation of finding oblivion in her body again. And he'd done it every day since. Three days…

And still he burned.

His lust undiminished.

She stirred beneath his fingers. Her eyes obscured by her hair, she smiled into the pillow. 'Did you have a nice shower?' she asked.

He removed his hand from her skin. 'I did.'

Pushing the hair from her eyes, she peeped up at him from beneath lowered lashes.

'You've shaved,' she declared.

Reaching out, she placed her fingertips to his cheek, swiped them down to meet his jaw. He caught her wrist gently, so as not to expose how her touch affected him. Hardened him. Mocked him for his lack of control. He pulled her fingers away and brought her knuckles to his mouth, brushed them against his lips.

Briefly, he closed his eyes.

Regained control of himself.

But the loss of his sight increased the scent of their shared arousal, coating the sheets, her skin…

His eyes opened and there were hers. Bright. Trusting. He placed her hand on the bed and handed her his neatly prepared list.

She had been so sure that their passion wouldn't burn itself out—and she'd been right. He'd known she would be. But he'd also known that it had to end once they reach Sicily. Once they reached their new home.

His chest was heavy, tight, and he kept his eyes on the piece of paper between them.

The storm outside was over, and now he'd contain the one inside him—whatever it took.

'It's time to leave, *piccolina*.'

'We're leaving?' Flora asked as she reached for the paper he was holding out to her.

'As soon as you are ready,' he confirmed.

Gripping the sheet between her fingers, she sat up, pulling it to cover her breasts, and took the paper from him.

'Lovely penmanship!' She flashed her teeth. 'I write like a toddler,' she confessed. 'Is it a letter? Numbered to count the ways you—?'

'No,' he interrupted, before the word *love* teased through her lips and presented itself, and he pushed the paper closer towards her.

'Okay. Someone needs some coffee…'

'I've had several.'

'Over-caffeinated?' she murmured under her breath, and focused on the flicks and twirls of his handwritten note.

She tucked her hair behind her ears. 'It's a list.' She frowned at him. 'What do we need this for?'

'Read it.'

Her eyes swept over the numbered bullet points on the list dated today: *dress-fitting, hair-stylist, photographer, wedding—*

'You want to get married *today*?'

'It's all arranged. We will arrive in Scarlata in three hours. Everything will be at the house waiting for us. Hairstylists. Flowers…' He shrugged. 'Tonight we will be married, and tomorrow—' He dipped his head to the list in her clenched fingers.

She followed his gaze. Ran through the next bullet points, the following week mapped out for her, marking each day's events. A nicely scripted list of what he expected her to do with her life.

'The doctor?' she asked, her eyes searching for the man he'd been last night.

But his face was a mask of shadows she didn't understand. Cloaked in an air of finality…

Raffaele nodded. 'That list comprises all the things that must be done before our new life can begin.'

'But…' She swallowed down on the anxiety bubbling in her chest. 'I haven't even chosen a dress.'

'A dress is a dress,' he dismissed evenly.

'My mum would like to see it,' she said. '*I* would like to see it. To choose—'

'Choices will be available for you. Your mother will see photographs,' he said, and her eyes widened.

After everything she'd told him of her family, the importance of her parents to her—had he forgotten? It was as if she'd never said it. Hadn't told him about her lack of choices growing up.

'The photographer—' he pointed to the list '—number three,' he said, redirecting her gaze, 'will be there when the team gets you ready for the church.'

'Church?' she echoed.

For a week there had been no routines, no carefully executed plans, and yet here he was, presenting one to her with a documented list of how she was to spend her life. Without her input…

'The church in Scarlata,' he said. 'It's small. The building has been an ongoing restoration project for many years.' He looked at the list, and she looked at him. 'Our nuptials,' he continued, 'will be documented. For our child. But you can present the pictures to your family as well. It will be as if they were there with us.'

'And who *will* be there?'

'Only you and me,' he answered.

'Because we're the only ones that matter?'

'It is a legal binding. To give our child protection. *My* protection. Nothing else matters,' he dismissed.

'Then why a church?' she asked. 'Why not some office?'

'When our child is grown—'

She halted him with a raised hand. 'The

church, the dress, the photographer…' She pulled the sheet tighter around her. 'Is all this for a baby who doesn't have a name yet?'

'It will have *my* name,' he corrected. 'And so will you. By the end of today you will be my wife,' he said. 'Signora Flora Russo.'

'And we'll spend the first day of our marriage in a doctor's surgery?'

'We have spent the last three days in bed—'

'Not all the time,' she rejected—because they hadn't. He had shown her the heights her body could reach in his arms. But he'd also held her in the dark, close to his body, folded her into the curve of his hips, and listened to her whisper stories of her life.

'These last three days—'

'Were what?' she asked, before she could stop herself. The words vibrated in the air between them.

'A step out of time,' he clarified. 'The honeymoon is over, Flora. It's time to focus on what matters.'

'And what's that?'

'The baby.'

They'd spent three days together without rules, without lists. They'd explored one another without restraint. But now it seemed that it was time to learn new rules. New routines. As Raffaele's wife. As Signora Flora Russo.

And she didn't know how she felt about it. The list...

His restraint laced through his cleanly shaved jaw. He'd downloaded the list that he'd written in his head seven days ago and nothing had changed. Not for him. While for her...

He hadn't learnt a thing. She was a bad teacher. She should have been able to share with him that she loved him. And he should have told her he loved her. Should have asked her to prepare this list with him—do it *together*. But he'd done it without her. Without any consideration of her feelings. The last three days hadn't diminished their desire, but she hadn't been able to show him that he could let it control him beyond that.

These things on this list were all about him getting control back.

That wasn't love.

Flora swept her gaze over the man on the edge of the bed. So close and yet so far. He was a shadow of that vulnerable man in the storm— the fierce lover he'd been since...

Had their time together meant nothing?

Was he still searching for the control he hadn't had trapped beneath that tree? Did he feel trapped with her? Was this list his escape? By leaving the boat and heading back to reality he could regain control without the chaotic input of emotion, of passion?

Flora would let him have it. The control. For now. Because she was too overwhelmed to do anything else or consider what this shift in mood meant. What his list meant for their future.

Flora did what she always did when she was doubting her feelings—her choices—and the chaotic emotions in her chest. She ignored them and followed the script.

'Okay,' she said, and laid the list on her lap. 'Number one: pack!'

The following hours moved at breakneck speed. Flora showered, dried, and dressed in an ankle-length coral skirt and matching full-sleeve top, with the daintiest buttons down the front. Her newly gained wardrobe was packed and presented to her in new leather suitcases. Three of them and a laptop case. A new tan leather shoulder bag. Her new phone.

And now they were all settled into the helicopter.

To take her towards her new life.

But she'd kept the list in her pocket. Folded into a perfect square beside her thigh.

The thigh that was millimetres from Raffaele's.

The thigh that did not move as they flew towards land.

Sicily.

They flew over peaked mountain hillsides full of olive groves and windswept trees. Above coastal towns, gleaming white, beside the sea. And as they moved deeper inland they were silent, both of them. Not speaking a word as reality got closer and closer.

The reality of marriage. Of suits and dresses. Of weddings and lists. Of a script penned by Raffaele for her, and for a baby that wasn't here yet.

But *they* were here.

He hadn't reached for her hand. Even though today he wasn't flying. He sat beside her, frozen as a statue. Untouchable.

The pilot's voice infiltrated the cabin. There was the village of Scarlata.

She looked down with bated breath and saw a village sandwiched between soaring mountains. Red-roofed houses, shops, cafés with tables dotted outside and fairy lights on every door, every window. It was a hub of activity. Of beauty.

She broke the silence. 'How long has it been since you've been back?' she asked.

He gave a cursory glance at the view. 'Never.'

'What do you mean, *never*?'

'After I sold the retreat…' he pointed down to a house in the middle of the square '… I never had any reason to go back to the village. I pumped money in when I could, and had people do what needed to be done to create the vision that I had for Scarlata, for its people. It's now a sought-after tourist destination. They didn't need me to oversee them fulfilling their destiny.'

'And your mother?'

'I paid people to do what needed to be done for her,' he said stonily. 'I came back to her when my father died, broke the news to her, and paid someone else to deal with the aftermath.'

'The aftermath?' she asked, but he didn't answer.

Flora's stomach flipped as they flew up the hillside to the land above it...as she saw what was built there.

'Is that your house?'

His eyes unreadable, he replied, 'It will be.'

'It's beautiful!' she gasped, extending her neck so she could admire its architecture. Tall white walls, intricately patterned columns, verandas, balconies on each floor with stone table and chair sets, climbing trellises of green foliage that ascended to a steepled roof...

And behind it the background was stunning. A forest of trees in greens and browns, and more mountains.

'This is where you grew up?' she asked, turning to him as the helicopter landed in a clearing marked with a big H.

'The only thing that remains of the house I grew up in are the foundations. Everything else—' he dipped his broad shoulders in a shrug '—is brand-new.'

'But you lived *here*?'

'With my mother.'

'Did she like it?' she asked.

'Like what?'

'How you transformed it?' Flora said, trying to imagine growing up here. What it had been like before he'd rebuilt it. 'The house? This isn't the home of a boy struggling to find food.'

'No,' he agreed. 'It is the house of the billionaire who rebuilt it. It was never my home, but it will be now.'

He unbuckled his belt and reached for hers.

Palms forward, she halted his touch. 'I can do it,' she said, and she did. Popped the buckle and untangled herself from the harness.

The proximity of their bodies belied the distance she could feel between them. He'd retreated somewhere inside himself, to a place she couldn't follow. Even his touch felt different. The hand at the base of her spine as he'd reached to help her had been incidental, courteous.

He felt different. Restrained. When the last three days he had been anything but.

'So did she?' she asked, focusing on him rather

than trying to organise her feelings. Admit what was happening.

His gaze narrowed. 'Did she what?'

'Did she like it? The house you built for her?'

'She didn't care.'

'Did you?'

'Did I what?'

'Care?' she pushed.

'About my mother?' he asked. 'Of course. I cared that the house she wanted to remain in was safe. That it had everything she could need and more. I built extra rooms, extended the floors to accommodate staff to cook, clean, watch her.'

'What do you think she would have thought about us coming here? Making it our home?'

'She probably wouldn't have noticed.'

'Your mother wouldn't have noticed that her son had brought home the woman he was going to marry?'

He shifted in his seat. 'They are waiting for us, *piccolina*.' He nodded towards the double oak doors.

Staff stood there. *Security guards?* Men in black suits and sunglasses.

'You need security?' she asked. 'Here?'

'I'm a billionaire, Flora. I need security everywhere, and so will you,' he said tightly.

'You didn't have any at the hotel.'

'And look what happened.'

'You didn't have any on the boat.'

'We were in the middle of the sea.' He exhaled deeply. 'You are stalling,' he declared. 'Why?'

'Because once I step off this helicopter I won't see you again until we make our vows—promises.'

He frowned. 'And you've changed your mind?'

'Of course not. But…'

'But what?'

'Tell me something…' she started, and tried to swallow down the emerging reality of her future. Her shared future with this man. The personification of wealth and privilege. Cold self-control. 'Of all the places we could get married and build a home,' she continued, and placed her open palm on his thigh, 'why here, Raffaele?'

She felt the muscles tense beneath her hand. Her insides churned as she prodded to find the man beneath the suit. The man she'd slept with. Talked to. Eaten with. The man who had disappeared into the bathroom to have a shower and not come out.

'Why come back when your mum isn't here? Not once have I heard you call this house your home. Not once have I heard—'

His eyes blazed. 'Enough, *piccolina*,' he said between unmoving lips.

There he was. Simmering beneath the surface.

The man she'd fallen in love with. With that all-consuming energy pressing against his skin.

'Enough of what, Raffaele? Acknowledging the elephant in the room?'

Unflinching, she held his gaze steady, although she wasn't sure it was the right move. Her rational brain told her to get out of the helicopter and fall into the hands of the people Raffaele had arranged to get her ready for a wedding.

To follow the plan.

The script for her wedding.

When she hadn't even seen the dress.

Hadn't even seen the church where the ceremony would take place.

And she wasn't sure if she was marrying the man who'd shared a bed with her last night or this man beside her who was fighting her. Fighting the status quo they'd created of touching freely, expressing themselves with words, kisses, intimacy.

'If it's so hard to be back here—' she said.

'It's not *hard*.'

'You're lying.'

'And you know this because you know me so well?'

'Maybe I don't know you at all,' she replied. 'I don't know the person you're trying to be right now.'

'Who am I trying to be?'

'Cold. Indifferent.'

'Maybe I *am* cold.' He looked straight through her. 'Indifferent.'

'You're neither of those things.'

He crossed his leg and flicked at a piece of invisible lint. 'Am I not?'

'You're pretending you are,' she said, slowly joining the dots in her mind. 'Only with me you haven't been like that. Not in London. Not on your boat. Only here.'

'How do you know I haven't been pretending all this time just to get you here?'

'Because I know,' she said without hesitation.

The man beside her was a lie, and the truth she'd experienced with him had been too honest, too raw, for it to come from anyone other than the man he hid beneath his suit.

'I was there with you. Making promises in the storm. And now that we're not there you're pretending you've forgotten that we promised each other to give the chaotic chemistry between us a home if we couldn't burn it out.'

He picked up the hand on his thigh and placed in on hers. 'But it *has* burnt out—like a pinched flame, *piccolina.*'

'No, I can feel it still simmering between us. This charge…' She swallowed down the hurt of his unexpected rejection. 'You're running from it,' she declared. 'Hiding from me…from yourself. And I'm done with running from the elephant in the room.' She sat straighter, taller. 'Stop lying,' she demanded. 'To me. To yourself. Because I'm not going in there until I understand what's happening between us. What's changed. Why we're here.'

'You can't refuse to get out of a helicopter every time we travel in one,' he hissed.

'I can do what I want,' she countered, heat flushing all the way up from her chest to heat her face. 'It's called being a grown-up. Facing the situation presented to you and gathering all the facts, whether or not you want to learn them. Don't redact the truth with me—I never want to be in the dark again. That list…it overwhelmed me. But I've got myself together now. I've remembered who I am. The woman I want to be. I want to face the facts—all of them—right here and now. Don't you?'

He didn't speak for the longest time. Didn't move.

'*Tell* me,' she said, her throat dry. Her brain was twisting itself to understand the information he was hiding from her. Find the facts. 'Explain why we're here? Why is it so important to you to have your new family—*me*—in a home where you never knew any genuine sense of family… where you were never shown love, only rejection?'

With a slight shake of his head, Raffaele closed his eyes briefly. 'We have spoken about origins, Flora. Knowing our roots.' He shrugged. 'These are mine. This house was once a place to be avoided. The people inside unimportant. Insignificant. Now it is a beacon of privilege. It is because of *this* house that Scarlata pulses with life. When our baby grows,' he said, keeping his eyes on the house, 'the strength of what its father has become will outweigh the whispers I once endured. Our child will be strong because of these roots. *My* roots. This house that was once nothing more than a shell will be a family home.'

He turned to her then.

'*Our* home, *piccolina*. I don't want this love you talk of. I wouldn't thrust it upon anyone—especially our child. I've seen first-hand how love manipulates. Breaks those it claims to care for irreparably.'

'Your mum?'

'Love broke my mother. The lie of it. The illusion. She waited all her adult life for love to return to her, and when it didn't—when her love died—she chose to end her life.'

Horrified, she let her hand fly to her mouth. 'Love ended her life?'

'No. Love doesn't exist. It was the illusion of love that killed her,' he confirmed, his tone flat. Emotionless.

'What about her love for you?'

'She didn't love me. She provided a bed. A roof.'

'The same things you're offering me?'

'No, I am offering you what I have offered from the very beginning,' he answered. 'Nothing has changed.'

'*I've* changed.' She placed a hand on her chest. 'Inside.'

'We did as you suggested. We burnt out the fire. We know one another. Know why we're entering this marriage.'

'I don't understand what's happened…'

He tilted her chin between his thumb and forefinger, bringing their gazes in line with one another. 'I can touch you with control.'

But he couldn't. He might be desperate to believe that he could, but he hadn't been quick enough to conceal the flash of heat in his eyes.

'Lying again, Raffaele?' she challenged him, feeling her body instantly responding to *this* man. The truth in his eyes. The heat in them. The longing she recognised in him because it weighed down in her own stomach, pushing the heat lower.

'And what if I can't touch you the same way?' she asked.

'You must,' he insisted.

'Why?' she asked. 'Because you don't want

me? Don't want the woman you told me I could be—*should* be?' she corrected.

She saw his eyes glued to her lips, to the words spilling out of her because she couldn't stop them. Didn't want to stop them.

'I *feel*, Raffaele. I *want*. I'm a woman who needs *you*. Needs the man who collected me from the farm. The man I met in London. The man on the yacht.'

The grip on her chin tightened. 'This last week,' he said quietly—*roughly*. 'The storm… the explosions of emotion from you.' His nostrils flared. 'And from me,' he admitted. 'The turbulence of it—of us—has made me want…'

She saw that the admission had cost him. It was written on every granite line etched into his beautiful face.

'You want the exact opposite of what we could be?'

'And what do you *think* we could be, Flora?'

'Happy.'

'What happened on the boat wasn't happiness,' he snarled. 'It was sex.'

'And you've gone full circle back to being afraid of having sex with me?'

'It's not about fear. It's not about sex.'

'What *is* it about?' But just like that the penny dropped, and she answered for him, without pause. 'The baby.'

'It was only ever about the baby.' He released her chin. 'Our time on the yacht was a mistake. Now we move past it.'

'How?' she asked huskily.

'We go inside,' he said. 'We follow the list. We do the right thing for our child, the way our parents did not do it for us.'

She reached into her pocket. Let the crisp lines of the folded square of paper slip and slide in her grasp. She pulled it out and handed it to him. 'I don't need this,' she said. 'I don't want it. You don't need to pay people to look after me, Raffaele. I can look after myself.'

A pulse hammered in his naked jaw. Realisation punched her in the sternum. Trapping her breath into her lungs. Filling every sense with a feeling she recognised. Had lived with her entire life.

Fear.

She sucked in a breath and allowed herself to process her own wants, her own needs, and saw his. The needs he was trying to hide so desperately behind his suit. His billions. Behind the group of people he paid to take care of the things he didn't want to face in case he got it wrong.

But that was life. Getting it wrong and still choosing to live.

Now Flora saw this moment for what it was. What it meant to him. A man who hadn't been home since he was a boy to a house without his mother. He had left behind a village that he had lifted up. He had become vulnerable in the beginning of a storm because of his memories.

She dropped the list on the floor. His gaze lingered it on it. Her hand rose and she gripped his chin between her thumb and forefinger, as he'd done to her.

'I want us to leave this helicopter without fear,' she said.

'I am not—'

'Shh…' she said gently, and watched his lips stretch and thin. 'I want you to choose to be the man you are with me, because I'm not going anywhere without him. We are going to go into that house and make it a home. Fill it full of feelings. *Our* feelings. We can write our own history, starting now, if you trust your instincts the way you showed me to trust mine. It frightened me in the storm. Frightened me that I'd made all the wrong choices and that the woman I was becoming was the wrong woman for me to be. It was the feeling of fear I've had since you came back to me.'

'And now the fear is gone?'

'Because of you.' She leaned in, bringing her mouth millimetres from his. 'You let me talk, feel, touch. Explore myself without judgement.

However chaotic—however illogical my feelings were…'

She flicked her tongue over her trembling lips.

'You showed me the man you are.' She stroked a hand across the tightness of his left shoulder. 'The man beneath this suit. I need to be claimed by *that* man. The man desperate to be inside me. Because he has wants—needs—just like me. He isn't cold or indifferent. Choose to be *him*. If you want to be with me, choose instinct, Raffaele. Let go of the list.'

She feathered her lips against his and he trembled against her.

'Let go of this façade the way you did in the storm. Because I see you, Raffaele,' she said. 'And you see me. So let's not stop looking at each other *now*, when everything is about to change.'

She pulled away, dropping her hands from his body, and met the blazing ethereal blue of his.

'What do you want, Raffaele?'

For a long heartbeat he didn't move. Then he did. He bent down and picked up his handwritten list. He opened each fold with careful precision.

'I want to let go,' he rasped, and tore the list in two and let the pieces flutter to the floor. 'I want to let go of everything but *this*. But *you*.' He grasped her hand, threaded his fingers between hers. 'I want to marry you. I want this day to end with the woman you are being bound to the man you make me want to be.'

'For us?'

His Adam's apple bobbed above the knot of his tie. 'For *me*,' he said. 'Marry me because...'

Her breath hitched. 'Because...?'

'Because I can't imagine starting tomorrow without you in my bed. In my arms. I need you there. Beside me. *With* me.' He reached up, brushed his thumb along her cheekbone. 'Looking at me with those all-seeing brown eyes.' He gripped her face, pulled her into him, and asked, 'Will you marry me, Flora Bick?'

She closed her eyes and pressed her forehead to his. She pushed down her need for the words—for Raffaele to choose this moment to confess that this, what they were feeling, was love. He still wasn't ready. She was, but she would wait until he could hear the words. Understand that she wasn't an illusion. That her love wasn't a lie. They had fallen in love.

What if he can't hear it? Understand? What if he doesn't want to learn what this means?

She slammed the door on those questions because they came from a place of fear, and she wouldn't let fear chase her away from what she wanted ever again. Because the first time she had put fear aside she'd met him. And now they were going to be a family. *Her* family.

How could it be a bad thing to set aside all those raging doubts when they'd given her *him*?

Flora met his gaze. Both of them were searching, both looking. And she said, 'Okay.'

She swallowed the exhalation against her lips. The relief mirrored in her smile shook, but she smiled through it. Through any lingering doubt. This was the right decision.

'I'll marry you, Raffaele Russo.'

CHAPTER ELEVEN

'I HAVE COME HOME.'

Raffaele stared at the grave, yet to be marked with a tombstone. There was only a white cross, etched with her name.

Maria Russo

Flowers were delivered from the gardens surrounding the house every week, cut and collected by the hands of the people he paid to keep her company even in death.

He delivered them today. Placed the white-headed blooms on the deep rich soil.

At his request, she'd been brought home after the inquest into her death in Italy. Had been buried as she had lived and died—without him.

His guilt was heavy. Still. It sat on his shoulders and refused to loosen its grip, even on his wedding day.

He'd left the house unseen, his departure unnoticed, and walked through the knotted trees in his wedding suit with one of the white blooms in his buttonhole. He'd made his way down the hill on the outskirts of the village and walked to the church. Arriving at the back gate to the small graveyard.

To see his mother.

'I am getting married, Mamma,' he said now, to the winds, to the soil, to the earth that protected her.

To his mother.

'She is fierce,' he continued. 'This Flora Bick. She was hiding when I found her on the English coast. All jeans and pumps and cows. And still I saw her. *Shining.* But now she will wear ball gowns. Because she was born to do so, Mamma. She was born to walk into a room and shine the way you deserved to shine. In jewels, in dresses of silk, protected by a name of privilege. Protected and adored with my father's wealth. I'm sorry my wealth wasn't enough. I'm sorry I didn't give you the choice to grieve in your own home when the man you loved died and with him your dreams of reconnecting with him. I'm sorry I was the one to tell you he was dead, and I'm sorry that I didn't let you scream, cry, break things… I should have stayed with you. I never should have sent you to that private clinic, however esteemed it was. Because it was not where you wanted to be. But you found a way out, didn't you? A way to be with *him.*'

He shoved down the childish urge to ask her why *he* hadn't been enough to make her choose a different path out of that facility. Why she hadn't talked to the therapists provided there. Talked to *him*.

It didn't matter. This was idiotic. But he needed her to know that he had not forgotten her. And to tell her what would happen next.

'She wants me to do something—give her something I cannot. Because the rage—' he swallowed down the lump in his throat '—the regret… It's mine, isn't it? It belongs to me. And forgiveness is yours to give. But still you do not speak to me.'

Raffaele closed his eyes, listened to the rustle of the trees and the call of the crows high in their towers.

Otherwise there was silence.

Had he expected anything else?

'For years you told me you didn't want me. Didn't need me to bring home food. You didn't need me to brush your hair. Help you slide into the bath…'

His voice trailed off as he remembered her frailty. Her refusal to fight. And in the end he hadn't been strong enough to fight for them both.

'I didn't listen to you. I just kept brushing your hair. Kept trying to—'

He sucked it in. The frustration. The hotness

of it. The visceral kick to his guts, as strong as it had ever been, that he hadn't been able to save her from herself.

'I'm sorry I didn't listen to you. That I let your words get into my head and in the way of the duty I was bound to. And then I stopped brushing your hair.'

Every word he'd wanted to say for three months he said now. To whom, he didn't know. She was gone. This white cross… This soft overturned earth… They were nothing more than a shrine for mourners. This graveyard was for the living, not the dead. But he carried on talking because he couldn't stop.

'I will get married today, Mamma, and I promise you this: I will protect my family. I will never pay for someone to care for them for me. She will get my name. My wealth will protect her. But I will never give her this disease—this promise of love that destroyed you. I cannot love her. But I will turn your house into the home you were never given, the home you were denied. Know from this day that everything my father denied to you I will give to her. To my wife. I cannot claim your forgiveness, but my promise is my redemption. *She* is my redemption.'

He turned his back on the grave, his breathing fast and shallow, and stopped. Everything blurred into one image. One person. One woman.

Her brown hair was in an elegant chignon.
A pearl-tipped tiara sat in her hair. She wore a
wedding dress with long lace sleeves with an
intricately sewn pearl pattern down the length
of the arms…around her throat.

'How did you find me?'

She was his redemption?

Confirmed by a loveless vow promised to a
dead woman?

Flora's heart thumped wildly against the pearl
buttons of the boned bodice of her dress.

Her wedding dress.

Here she stood, outside the church she was
going to get married in, a bouquet in her hands
of every colour, listening to a man who was
promising never to love her.

And it hurt. It was palpable. His rejection of a
love she hadn't voiced. Already it was unwanted.

Her love.

And by God, she wanted to touch him. Grab
him by the shoulders and tell him to open his
ears, his heart. Tell him he was wrong, and that
all the things he'd promised to his mother—to
provide for his wife—she didn't want them. Any
of them. She didn't care about his money. His
name. His protection. She wanted the unconditional love her parents had raised her with. She
wanted to love him unconditionally and wanted

it in return. Wanted to fill their house with love, not…*things*.

Instead, she swallowed her words down deep, until they lodged themselves in her chest to remain unspoken. Because they wouldn't matter. She knew that because he was not ready to let go of the woman whose grave lay behind him. Because he had not forgiven himself for her death.

She had no clue what the right words to say were. But she knew they shouldn't be about her. Because this was firmly about him.

So she trusted her instinct, lifted one flat white pump and trod onto the mossy grass, brought herself closer to him. To the man now frozen in the graveyard, looking at her as though he'd conjured a ghost.

She reached him, stood before him. His breathing was audible, the heavy rise and fall of his chest rapid. Flora placed her hand on his chest and looked up into his eyes. His face was the sculpted face of a mystic. Dark. Tortured.

'I followed you, of course.' She smiled tightly. 'We're getting married, aren't we?'

Reaching down, she caught his hand and gave his tight fingers a quick squeeze. Then she nodded and stepped beside him, knelt down. The hem of her dress disappeared into the grass.

She spoke to Raffaele's mum.

'Signora Russo,' she started, 'I promise to always follow my instinct and guide your son to make the best choice for *him*. I hope this brings you peace.'

She took her bouquet in both her hands and pulled it apart, separating it into two parts. Then she laid half of the dainty rainbow-coloured flowers beside the white ones already there.

She stood, turning her back on the grave. 'Ready?' she asked.

'For what?' he asked huskily.

'You wrote the list.' She tapped her wrist and pointed to an invisible watch. 'It's time.'

'Why did you follow me?'

'I saw you leave. And I saw an opportunity to escape the photographer taking endless pictures of me being plucked and pruned and I broke free.'

He flinched. 'In your wedding dress?' he asked, his voice a broken husk of accusation. 'You could have hurt yourself.'

'*You're* in your wedding suit.'

It was a suit lighter in tone than the grey one he'd worn to travel in that morning. A thick Windsor knot was tied at his throat. There was a flower in his buttonhole. And he was beautiful.

But he was not ready, was he? To claim a wife. To love a family.

'I still can't wear heels.' She lifted the hem of

her dress and gave him a glimpse of her white-stockinged calves. 'The walk was easy enough.'

'You didn't call out? Didn't tell me you were there?'

'I assumed you'd be making your way here, to the church, and I wanted to be with you—not in a fancy car with strangers. I thought, *If we're doing this, we should do it together. Go inside together and get married.*'

'That is not the way this works.' His eyes narrowed. 'I'm supposed to be inside. Waiting for you.'

'I thought this could be *our* way.' She held out her hand, palm forward. 'Shall we…?'

'But the photographer…' he said.

'He doesn't matter,' she dismissed.

'The pictures?' he said. 'For your mother?'

'We'll have photos taken later,' she said.

His eyes darted to the hem of her dress, her scuffed white pumps. 'Your dress…'

'It doesn't matter.'

'Then what *does* matter?' he asked.

And this time her smile faltered. Flashed with the uncertainty on the edge of her thoughts. She wanted to say it was love that mattered. But she needed him to see, to understand that *he* mattered too. So very much to her. That she would take care of him when he was putting everything but himself on the list.

'Trusting yourself to write new rules,' she said, her chest tight. 'With me standing right beside you.'

Her hand, unclaimed, trembled in the air.

'Trusting myself?' he echoed.

'Let's write a brand-new script. Walk into that church by ourselves, *for* ourselves, together. Just you and me. I'll give myself away because you'll be there, claiming me, just the way I'll claim you.'

His hand rose from his side, reached out, and there in the graveyard their fingertips met. He pulled her in and she reached out for his shoulders. He gripped her waist and looked down into her face as she looked up into his.

'Together?'

She nodded. Did he get it now? Did he understand?

'Side by side, Raffaele. Through those doors, up the aisle, to say the words, vows, and promises to the only people that matter. The people getting married. *Us.*'

His chest heaved against hers. He dipped his head. But she didn't look at his lips. Didn't let herself feel the warmth of his breath on her lips. Because it wasn't a time for kisses. It was a time for words.

'Let go, Raffaele, and put all that rage and regret inside you into something new. You can't build on rotten foundations—so let's rip them out. Start again. Start again with me. Right now. Start something that's ours. Nothing to do with the past and everything to do with the future.'

His fingertips pressed into her hips and she felt the fight in his body. The battle between duty and the temptation of what she was offering. A life where they mattered to each other. Made choices *together*.

This time she didn't resist. She inched in at the same time he did. Their lips met. Held. Pressed to each other. A promise? A vow?

He grasped her hand tightly and pulled away. 'Let's get married, *piccolina*.'

Step by step they walked up the path leading to the front of the church. Hand in hand they turned the corner. And then—

Applause.

It burst the silence with a thrum of a hundred clapping hands and smiling eyes.

A man in an ill-fitting suit stepped forward. The gasp she heard from Raffaele's lips pushed every hair on her body into an upright position.

'Matteo...' Raffaele's said.

And the man pulled him into a tight embrace and held him against him for longer than was customary in any tradition, whispering words she couldn't hear into his ear.

Raffaele closed his eyes, and she felt the surge

of emotion in the hand clasping hers. The man stepped back, stood eye to eye with Raffaele, and both men nodded.

The man Matteo turned his attention and his smile to her. Kissed her heartily on both cheeks and squeezed her hand. And so it went on. Embraces and kisses. But not once did Raffaele let go of her hand, as side by side they moved through the crowd.

The community.

The community who had saved the boy who'd pulled them up in the world.

Who loved the man the boy had become.

And Flora felt it in every hug. Every handshake. Each heavy tap on the shoulder.

He'd always been loved.

He'd just never understood it.

Pulled along by grasping hands, they stood at the entrance of the church. An arch of green foliage with red, violet and white flowers surrounded the double oak doors.

The doors opened.

Hand in hand, they stepped inside.

'Raffaele…' she whispered, frozen in the face of such awe-inspiring beauty.

White silk and huge bouquets dressed every pew. There were long-stemmed flowers between candles that flickered throughout the space, and she felt as if she had stepped out of one time and into another.

On cue, the sun streamed through the high arched stained-glass windows on either side of them. Reflecting on every stone surface in a canvas of colour.

Tears filled her eyes. 'It's beautiful…'

The long, slow melodic swipe of a bow against a violin string whispered across the stillness of the church.

'Look up,' he said, his voice a throaty whisper.

Flora looked up at the stone-columned balcony above them. 'A string quartet?'

As if on cue, a vocalist with pink flowers in her hair stepped forward, began to sing 'Ave Maria'.

'It's time,' he said.

She looked at him. At the man who had given her a night of freedom in London, chased her—hunted her—to the farm and made her not only confront the confirmation of her pregnancy but the woman she wanted to be. With him. She trembled. She had never felt freer than she did right now. She was trusting in her instincts. Was trusting herself to be herself. Because of him.

She stood taller, squared her shoulders. 'Are you ready?' she asked.

'I am ready, Flora Bick,' he said, a pulse flickering in his jaw, 'to end this day with you as my wife.'

'And you as my husband,' she replied.

Their threaded fingers clasped tighter and they stepped onto the red carpet leading to the altar.

Together.

And behind them the villagers took their pews as, hand in hand, Raffaele and Flora took centre stage and presented themselves to the priest who would bind them.

Flora feathered her fingers against Raffaele's cheek and held back the tears misting her view as she spoke the words of her heart. The words he needed to hear.

'I know there wasn't time for my family to be here,' she said. 'But I'm so glad yours could be.'

Her heart stuttered for the boy under the tree. Cold and alone. For the boy caring for his mother when she should have been caring for him. For the boy standing at those iron gates, refused entry to a heritage that was his by birth.

Her grip tightened on the hand in hers. They were joined in front of his people. His family. Because sometimes family was the love of strangers. Sometimes it was a village.

'Look at them,' she ordered, and his eyes left hers to move over their audience.

The huge stained-glass windows threw rainbow patterns on their unexpected guests.

'They're all here for you.'

Slowly, his eyes moved back to hers.

'And so am I,' she promised, and that was her vow. Her promise.

She hoped he heard it, and that in time he would understand it. Embrace it as fully as he'd made her embrace herself.

Family.

Love.

CHAPTER TWELVE

RAFFAELE COULD NOT release his hold on his wife and she had not let go of him. She'd stayed by his side since they'd left the church to thunderous applause.

The photographer had caught up with them at the ceremony, as had his security team, who had managed to lose two whole human beings.

The day had been…surreal.

The ghosts who had haunted him every day since his departure from the village were alive, and present on his wedding day.

His gut clenched. It was too perfect. This life was not meant for him. And yet here it was. A village cheering for him and his new bride, sending them back to their house. To a house that was to become a home.

His home.

He couldn't breathe.

He tugged the knot free at his throat.

'Are you okay?'

The voice was velvet against his prickling ear-drums.

'I will be,' he assured her roughly, and shrugged off his suit jacket.

Raffaele wanted out. Out of the car. Out of his suit. He wanted to present himself, on his knees, as the man she wanted. *Him.* Bound by the gold band on his finger by choice. *His* choice.

He was married. And he was taking her home. In a dirt-rimmed wedding dress and mud-caked leather shoes. He wanted her out of the dress, too. He wanted to strip it from her body and reveal the softness he yearned for. Craved so desperately it hurt in his bones. He wanted to sink inside her and lose himself . Ignore the conflict in his chest. These warring emotions he couldn't name. Didn't want to.

Because if he did everything would disappear. She would vanish.

Breathless, they sat beside each other in the back of the luxury car. Breathing ragged. *Tight.* Staring at each other.

'Kiss me,' she demanded, and her eyes begged for him to do exactly what he wanted to do. Climb between her thighs and possess her.

He hooked his jacket onto the clip. 'I will not consummate our marriage in a car, Signora Russo.' His voice was tight. Not his own.

'Why not, Signor Russo?'

Her brown eyes flashed, molten, and he was melting under the onslaught. Caught in her challenging gaze.

'No one can see us,' she said. 'The windows are tinted. No one will hear us behind the privacy glass.'

'We'll be back at the house in—'

'I want you here,' she interrupted. 'I want you *now*. The only reason you could have for not doing what we both want is because you're scared.'

'Scared?' he growled. 'Never.'

But the lie tasted foul in his mouth. His body instantly rejecting his confident conformation. It didn't feel real. Any of it. This illusion she'd created of his life that he was wanted. Needed. By a community he'd thought had forgotten him.

She had challenged him every step of the way to confront the demons inside him. To tell them, as she had told his mother, that he should focus on his needs. His wants. What was good for him and no one else. Should bury his skeletons and rebuild a brighter future without fear. Let go of everything he'd held on to for thirty years…

And she'd be there when he did. Standing beside him. Holding his hand. He was not a child—he did not need a guide. But he needed *her*. What did that mean? Could they make this marriage work? Was it possible to have passion and commitment and family even if he couldn't offer her everything she wanted? Would Flora accept that?

He didn't know if this woman—*his wife*—was good for him. Or if he was bad for her.

'Show me,' she dared him. 'Make love to your wife.'

She reached for the small rounded pearl buttons and popped one free. Then another. Another... Revealing the swell of her white lace-covered breasts. She reached down to the hem of her skirt and folded it up, inch by inch, revealing her legs, then the bare flesh above her stockings, until the skirt sat on her hips.

He couldn't tear his gaze away. Her actions penetrated the heart of him. She *knew*. Recognised the chaotic *want* in him that wouldn't diminish. His undisguised need to be inside his wife. The chemistry he'd failed to deny between them. And here it was, demanding a place, a home, in their marriage.

'Love me, Raffaele.'

In that moment, he let go.

Her head fell back against the leather headrest and he devoured her neck. Licked the crevices behind her ear and worked down. Sucking, biting, until he got to her half-open bodice, found the tops of her breasts.

'You're beautiful…' His eyes caught and held the blazing brown of hers.

'I need you, Raffaele,' she said huskily, her mouth parted, gasping for him with a rawness he felt in the hardening swell of his body.

And she was calling for him to answer it. Their shared hunger. To release the emotions, the feelings, burning in his chest and let her taste them. Swallow them.

He roared and claimed her lips urgently, thrusting his tongue inside her mouth and ripping the dress from her body. His hands sought out her lace-covered breasts, pulled the lace down until his palms found her hardened peaked nipples and squeezed. He tilted his hips and pushed his throbbing length to her core.

Her small hands were on his belt, unbuckling him with swift fingers. She reached for the zip, pulled it down and reached inside.

'Flora!' He moaned her name fiercely as she took the velvet length of him in her hand and stroked him.

She placed a hand on his chest and pushed him away from her mouth. 'Sit down,' she ordered, and he grappled with his own tongue.

She pushed her breasts against his still-clothed chest, pushing harder until their positions were reversed and she sat between his thighs, his erection hard and pulsing between them.

She moved and straddled him. He gripped her thighs as she lowered herself onto him. He stared into her eyes because he couldn't look away. He didn't want to. Because this familiarity between them—this *knowing*—had always belonged to them, hadn't it? From the very first night they'd met...

She sank down, filling herself with the thickness of him deep inside her. 'Now...' she breathed, and her hips rose, teasing his length at her entrance, and then pushed back down.

'Flora...' he said huskily, because the pressure was building inside him with every lift of her hips and...

He thrust up his hips and she braced herself with a hand on the car's ceiling as she screamed his name. 'Raffaele!'

She pushed down, and he thrust again, until their synchronised rhythm was frantic. Chaotic.

'Harder!' she gasped, panting her need into existence. The need that mirrored his own.

He gripped her hips. Thrust harder.

Her hand on his jaw tightened, refusing to let him look away. And he looked at her—saw her for what she was—and stared at her in awe. In amazement. Mesmerised by her wide eyes. Her gasping mouth. Her innocence. And he matched her thrust for thrust, arching his hips to allow her to take him deeper in a reverse image of the night they'd met.

A deep blush bloomed on her neck…her cheeks. He could feel the heat radiating from her. The hotness filling the air between them with humidity—trapping them both inside it. Inside the bubble of desire they hadn't been able to deny the night they'd met in the shadows. And neither could they deny it now, in marriage and in the day's light. In the real world where they would live. Together.

'It's your turn to come for me, *piccolina.*' He pushed his hand between their joined bodies and applied pressure to her swollen nub. 'Let go,' he commanded, as she had him.

She clenched around him, squeezed, until they both roared their release into the air between them and let go together…

Breathing hard, she collapsed on top of him, her face buried in the crook of his neck. He cupped the back of her head and held her against him. The realness of her. This mystical woman who'd appeared in his life and filled every moment with…*magic.* Opened the door to a world he'd never thought possible. Not possible for him. She wanted to drag him inside to a place where family lived.

'I love you, Raffaele.'

His fingers loosened their grip on her.

The bubble popped.

Just as he had known it would.

Because this life was not his to claim. And neither was she.

He could lie. Whisper words of love. Convince her of the illusion of it the way his father had convinced his mother. He could keep her prisoner with his love. A love that would never come.

Or he could set her free.

She rose on his lap, held his gaze, and waited for him to repeat her words. Her lie.

So he made his choice. The only choice he could.

'I cannot love you back.'

Flora had expected it. His denial. And she smiled through the rejection because she knew the truth.

She loved him and he loved her.

She climbed off his lap and sat beside him, this man who had turned from fire to ice with those three little words. She fixed her bra, pulled the ripped seams of her dress together, and waited.

She was ready. Ready to teach a man who'd never known love how to accept it.

Raffaele tucked himself away and straightened his clothes, then turned to her, a pulse pounding in his bristled cheek.

'I can never love you,' he said, his face unreadable.

'What makes you think you don't already love me?' she asked gently.

'Because love doesn't exist. This is sex, Flora. A chemical connection in order to procreate.'

'But I'm already pregnant, so why do we keep making love?' she asked. 'Because you love—?'

'Because I enjoy sex, and I enjoy having it with you. Desire is natural.'

'And love isn't?'

'Love is a myth used to manipulate the weak.'

'I'm not weak, and neither are you.'

She placed her hand on his thigh and gave the tight muscles a squeeze. She watched him looking at the hand on his grey-covered thigh. Saw the debate flickering across his taut features. His hand moved. Reached for hers and hesitated. A palpable pause. Then he picked up her hand and placed it on her lap and turned his unwavering gaze to hers.

Flora held up her hand and pre-empted his rebuttal with a shake of her head. 'I'm aware that eavesdropping is a sin, but I will pay the price—because everything I heard you say to your mother I already knew. You only confirmed it.'

'Confirmed what?'

'That you don't know what love is.'

'I know exactly what it is,' he rejected. 'It is a myth. A lie.'

She shook her head. 'All your life you've been told stories of the man who promised to love your mother, promised to come back to her, and rejected her in the most callous way. He hid you both in a village that was nowhere in anyone's consciousness. He left you both to survive on the lie that he'd come back. That isn't love.'

'I never said it was.'

She ignored him. Because she understood him now. Understood his avoidance of anything other than providing the essentials. Food. Warmth. Shelter. But never love. Because he'd only ever experienced a kind of love that would have broken the strongest of men.

'Your father tricked your mother into thinking his seduction was love,' she continued, trying her hardest to keep her voice level. 'He lied to her and she believed him. And she made you believe too, in some distorted view of love.'

He was looking at her, but she knew he was somewhere far away. His eyes were…haunted.

'Why was she in so much pain if it wasn't love?' he asked between gritted teeth.

'Love isn't pain.'

She wanted to reach for him. Hold his hand and ask him her next question.

She resisted, and continued, 'Was that when the doctors diagnosed her with depression?'

'Yes,' he hissed heavily. 'And medicated her.'

She nodded. 'She wasn't well, Raffaele. She was sick and she was relying on a little boy to carry her pain for her. She focused all her energy on the wrong place. The wrong person. Because her attention should have been on you. She pretended she'd had a great romance with an Italian noble—but her romance was a tragedy. It wasn't love. Her happily-ever-after was never coming—but ours can. If we trust in what we're feeling.'

That pulse pounded in his cheek. He was coming back to her from wherever he'd gone. Into the past? But would he hear her? Understand?

She pushed on. 'That storm took you both to hospital—it saved her and broke you when it should have given you every urge to live life without restraint. It should have told you she wasn't accountable for her lack of love. Her lack of care for you when she couldn't care for herself. Love doesn't hurt. I won't hurt you,' she promised. 'So let me love you. And admit,' she said, 'that you love me too.'

'I don't,' he said roughly. 'I don't love you.'

'Wanting to take care of someone *is* love, Raffaele,' she insisted. 'Keeping them safe. Feeding them breakfast in the afternoon because they skipped it that morning. It's looking for someone in a storm because you need to know they're safe. It's Matteo,' she said, as the memory of the man's name jolted a memory of what he'd told her about the storm.

Matteo had rescued him.

'Matteo the bar-owner,' she continued, 'showed up at your wedding, with all the villagers at his back, to see the boy he rescued from a storm living his life. They *all* came to see you get married.'

'It was just respect for what I did for them—'

'No,' she rejected, her voice a harsh rasp. 'It was for *you*. Love is lots of things, but most of all it's actions.'

She steeled herself for the next part. For the bit that would hurt him the most. She was going to rip off the plaster and make him hear it.

'Love is a little boy brushing his mother's hair when all she wants to do is sleep.'

'How could I have loved her, Flora?' he whispered. 'As soon as I could, I left her. I only came back when I learned of my father's death. I didn't want her to be alone when she found out.'

'Because of what might happen?' she asked quietly.

'It happened anyway,' he said. 'I came back. I told her. And she died. Because as soon as I'd told her I left again and paid other people to look after her. To hear her cries. Her screaming that this was not how it was supposed to be. He promised he'd return, but now he was dead. I left her alone in her grief and she ended her life. If love was all the things—the *actions*—you say it is, I would have stayed and watched her with my own eyes. Not paid for doctors to care for a woman they couldn't protect.'

'It was never your job to protect her from herself,' she told him. 'Your mother made her own choices. Choices you'll never understand. Just like I will never understand why my mother gave me up for adoption.'

'They are not the same thing,' he snarled, teeth bared.

'You're right. They're not. Because I grew up with a family that loved me. I understand all the choices they made now. Because love *is* wanting to protect your own. Your family. Did they always get it right? No. But I understand it now. I understand it was love that pushed them to decide what they did.'

'I failed my mother because of *my* decisions and now she is dead,' he said. 'Because of me. Because I looked away. *That* is not love.'

He closed his eyes. Shut her out. And she let him.

He laid his head back against the headrest. 'What is your compulsion to have life-changing conversations in moving transport?'

'Instinct,' she replied. 'Because every time we've been in the helicopter, a car, I know that when we get out things will happen. And I want to decide with you—*together*—what happens next.'

He didn't open his eyes, but the fingers splayed on his spread thigh flexed.

'We could be in bed. We could be anywhere but here,' he said, his voice gruff, coming from somewhere deep in his chest.

'Still hiding from the elephant in the room?'

His eyes flew open. 'I am not hiding. I am answering your questions—your statements of love—truthfully, however much you might dislike my replies.'

'And then what will you be doing?'

'Everything I said I would,' he clipped.

She slapped straight back. 'In the storm on the boat you said you should never have put your re-action to the past on me. But you still are, Raffaele. I'm not your mother, and you're not your father. I don't know how to make you understand that this is love—'

'"This" is simple, Flora.'

'It is?'

'We will be lovers. Companions. Maybe even friends. And we will raise a baby together. But understand this…'

He shuffled closer to her. She could smell herself on his skin. Their shared arousal. The desire still simmering between them to be closer. To entwine their hands and touch each other. But he didn't touch her, so she wouldn't touch him either. She wouldn't hide in his kisses and she wouldn't let him hide in hers.

'Love will never find you in *that* house.'

He pointed out of the window to the house the car was now pulling up to. The house that would be her new home. He should be carrying her over the threshold to start her new life as Signora Russo.

'Because it never found you?' she asked quietly. 'I'm not your redemption for whatever guilt you feel about the past. I'm your wife, and I'm asking you to let me love you, to love me in return. Because that little boy deserved more than the kindness of strangers. He deserved to be loved and so do you.'

She placed her hand to his chest and everything in her told her to climb back onto his lap and hold him. Hold him until he understood that the love she gave him with her body came from her heart. Her soul.

'Love me, Raffaele,' she said. 'Trust yourself to love me. Now.'

She was asking him just as she had in the storm, but now she needed all his love. Not only his body. But his heart.

'I can't.'

She held the breath in her lungs. Let it burn. Let it stem the tears threatening to spill all over her cheeks.

She wasn't a very good teacher, it would seem. *One more lesson.* Her heart roared. *The hardest.*

And if it didn't work this love affair would be over and she'd raise her baby by herself. Surrounded with love that was unconditional. But she would give him one more chance to choose love. To choose family. To love her.

And he would choose her, wouldn't he?

She blew out the air between her lips and put the last lesson she had to teach into motion.

Pulling her hand from his body, she turned her eyes straight ahead. She said, 'Get out of the car, Raffaele.'

'What?' he growled.

She did not turn. She would not look at him. 'Why?'

'You said love won't find me in that house, so I'm not going in.'

'It's our wedding day, Flora.'

'And you have vowed never to love me. I won't raise my baby in a house without love.'

'Flora—'

'Get out.'

The silence rippled with tension, charged with everything she held back. This time on purpose—not because she was being illogical or chaotic. Because even if she said all those words, expressed all the thoughts in her head, she knew he wouldn't hear them.

She needed to show him.

'Where will you go?' he asked.

Forcing herself not to react, not to turn and ask him if it was really that easy to get out of the car and let her drive away, she kept her eyes forward and replied as neutrally as her raging heart would allow.

'To a place where love has always found me.'

She reached over him, eyes downcast, and refused to recognise the scent of him. She opened the door for him.

'I'm going home. The adventure is over.'

'You're pregnant—'

'Yes, and we will figure that out as we need to.'

She looked at him then. Watched his world ripple in confusion. But this was the only way she could help him. Make him understand that nothing else mattered but what he was willing to close the door on. What he was willing to sacrifice because of the little boy he once was, who wouldn't let the man he had become accept love because he didn't think he deserved it.

Eyes wide, he got out and stared back at her.

She knew he'd have to figure out how to fix this—if he wanted to—all on his own. Trust himself.

She made herself turn. Made herself look away. She was doing the right thing.

She rapped on the privacy glass until the driver opened it. 'To the airport, please, driver.'

The driver nodded, and the glass once again ascended.

'Flora, your dress…'

He was reminding her of the passion that only moments ago had torn through them both. She reached for his suit jacket, still on the hook, and put it on. Slid her arms into the silk-lined sleeves, pulled them over the intricate lace covering her arms. The jacket was still warm from his body.

She ignored it. She squared her shoulders. 'Goodbye, Raffaele.'

Only when she heard the click of the door did she let her shoulders sag. Let herself pant, sucking in the air she'd been denying herself. She twisted on the seat to sit up on her knees, looking out of the rear window. And there was her husband, standing on the gravel drive, letting his wife drive away.

He was letting her go.

She crumpled into a tearful mess on the back seat where she'd made love to her husband.

Because she was leaving him and she didn't want to.

CHAPTER THIRTEEN

THERE WAS MONEY in the pocket of the suit jacket that Flora has taken. Lots of it. Enough to buy her a first-class round-the-world ticket. She would find it. She'd be fine.

But will you?

It had paralysed him. Watching her, everything he'd chased after—*hunted*—driving away with his baby in her belly. His family.

Something had torn inside Raffaele with every crunch of the tyres driving over the gravel.

She'd asked him repeatedly to let go, and with his body he had. But she wanted him to let go with his heart. To *love*. And he couldn't let go with his heart because love had never been inside it. There was nothing inside it for her. For his baby.

Maybe this was the best choice. He would provide them with the protection of his name. Financially he'd give them anything, everything,

and he would never deny his child its roots…
its story.

Is this how your story ends? Stuck in this house? Prisoner of the past? With your future driving away?

He couldn't move. Not towards the house behind him, and not towards the car. He was stuck. Breaking inside. Was this his choice? To hold on to fear when Flora—?

She wasn't afraid, was she? Not of his failings—not even when he'd thrust the truth of his neglect at her. Her innocent eyes had still looked at him with hunger. With warmth. There had been softness in even her most hungry caress. She'd touched him with love.

Pain. It sliced through him. Acute. *Searing.*

The car had reached the end of the drive. Soon it was going to vanish out of sight, move down the hill on the road he'd had built into the mountain and drive out of his sight, out of his life.

He didn't think—he just ran. *Fast.*

His legs pumped along with the thud of his leather-sheathed feet on the uneven ground.

But the car didn't stop.

He wanted to roar. Demand her presence. So why didn't he? He knew her name. She was no longer anonymous. She was his wife. She had given him all of herself. All of her trust. All of her…

Love?

His chest heaving, he stood at the end of the drive and let go. Let go of the fear, of the past, and trusted his instincts. He roared his needs, his wants into the air and called out loud, fierce. He was a man calling for his mate. His love.

'Flora!'

Just as he was preparing to sprint down the hill the car stopped—and so did his heart. The car door opened. With bated breath he watched her climb out and stand there, looking at him at the top of the hill.

Then they both ran.

He ran so fast he felt as if he was flying. Running free towards the future. Towards love. *His destiny.* And he wouldn't look away.

He loved her. Loved her chaotic fierceness. Her innocence. He wanted every word he'd whispered to her about trusting herself to apply to him. He wanted to trust her. To believe that this was love and he deserved it. He wanted to be the man she'd made him. The man he was beneath the suit. The man he'd always been.

Because he wasn't trapped under a tree.

He wasn't lost any more.

He was *found.*

Their bodies slammed together. His fingers thrust into her hair and pulled her mouth to hers. And he kissed her with everything he was.

He kissed her for every year he hadn't felt loved. For every time he'd chosen control instead of his feelings. Put on his suit and written a list, pretending his feelings weren't involved.

She would make him feel. She would teach him to love openly, without fear. Just the way he was loving her now. In the open. In the gentle light of the late-afternoon sun.

Gripping her arms, he pushed her away from him and panted, 'Flora—'

'I know,' she soothed—and he knew she did. 'It's hard to trust it, isn't it?'

'Yes.'

'You'll get better at it,' she promised.

He swallowed heavily, still holding her tightly in place in front of him.

'I have never known family. I have never known love. But I want to learn. I want to love you. Be a family. Be in a marriage and be parents to our child. I want you for me—but I want this marriage for *us*. I want us to be a team. Do things for each other and with each other. I want to turn that house into a home with you. Not in redemption. I see that now. I understand that whatever choices I made, I couldn't choose for my mother. Her choices were her own, as mine are my own. I want to trust in my own decisions. Because how could I not when they have brought me to you? Will you let me love you, Flora? Will you let me practise my love on you every day?'

He fell to his knees.

'Will you be my wife?'

'I already am.'

She fell to her knees beside him and cradled his face, looked into his eyes, claiming his world as her own. Driving the flag in.

'I love you, Raffaele Russo.'

'It was always you,' he said. 'From the first night you broke open my chest and brought my soul, my heart, back to life. And that was love, wasn't it? Even then. Because you are my destiny.'

She stroked his face. 'Destiny,' she agreed.

'I love you,' he said, and he heard the tremble in his own voice. The release.

And then he gave in to what his body wanted, his heart wanted, and kissed her thoroughly there on the gravel driveway, until the only thing left to do was to pick her up and carry her over the threshold.

'I promise to turn this house into a home and fill it with love, Flora. *My* love.'

He looked down into her face and she looked back up into his. And there was the world. *His* world.

'I love you. I always did. I always will.'

EPILOGUE

'YOU'RE SO STRONG, Flora,' Raffaele said huskily, anticipation humming in his every muscle.

'I'm not…'

'You are.'

She closed her eyes and squeezed his fingers. He let her squeeze, let himself be the unbreakable strength she needed to beat against in order to bring new life into the world. A life *they* had made.

Flora had refused a private suite at the hospital. Refused to leave her home. *Their* home.

Why would she leave it to be surrounded by strangers when all she could ever want was right here? she'd said. Her family.

She wanted their baby to be born in their home. Here. In a room that sang with life. With love. A love she had injected into every surface, every wall, until the house he'd never considered a home had become his home because of her. Because she was in it.

He'd fought hard to trust her choice to bring their

baby into the world with only a midwife. He hadn't put every doctor in Sicily on standby. The air ambulance was not waiting in the gardens and the suite at the hospital was not prepared.

He was still learning to trust that love was actions, but he was practising and developing his skills every day. She was patient, but stern, and sometimes hot words turned to hotter kisses.

He *was* Sicilian after all.

And sometimes no words were needed at all. Because couples fought, he had learnt, but then they made love and made up. And they were a couple. They were a family. Every night he climbed into bed beside his wife and knew that this was where he belonged. By her side.

But right now he felt absolutely helpless. He wanted to take all the pain from her. But he couldn't. So he stood strong and rubbed her back. Kissed her forehead and placed water to her lips. He would love her in all the silent ways she'd taught him to love. Take care of her not only in the big ways, but the small ways too. Be present for her.

'*Raffaele...!*'

His gut clenched.

In thirty-six hours, every minute—every *second*—had been for this.

The last shout of his name.

The final push.

A wail erupted from a bundle of wrinkled skin topped with the darkest curly hair.

Raffaele looked at his wife—at her flushed cheeks, her damp brow. Her gasping mouth. His wife. His heart.

He turned back to the baby. His baby. His family. A miracle…

'Congratulations, Signor and Signora Russo. She's perfect.'

'A girl?' he croaked, feeling the lump in his throat growing.

The midwife smiled. 'With ten fingers and ten toes,' she clarified.

'She's really here…?' Flora's voice was a throaty expression of awe.

He nodded. Entwined their hands tightly. 'She's here,' he echoed.

Because she was. His daughter.

'Help me, Raffaele.'

'Of course!'

He turned to Flora, silently reprimanding himself for not anticipating her needs. She looked up at him, the smile on her lips tight but true.

'What do you need?' he asked.

'I need you to help me undo this…' She pulled at the fabric covering her. 'I want my baby on my chest.'

He placed his trembling hands on Flora's, also trembling, clumsily trying to undo the buttons of her nightdress.

'I'm so proud of you, *piccolina*,' he said, slipping each button through the hole which housed it.

His chest was full and bursting with so many feelings. Joy. Happiness. *Love.*

His task complete, he saw his wife reach for the hem of Raffaele's black tee.

'Take it off.'

Brows drawn together, he asked, 'Take what off?'

'Your T-shirt.' She tugged at it. 'Then get in bed and let's hold our baby for the first time together.'

He did as she requested. Slipped his T-shirt over his head. He didn't care if this was how things should be done. It was *their* way.

He climbed into bed beside his wife. Flora held out her hands, arms outstretched. 'We're ready.'

Their naked baby was placed on Flora's bare chest by the steady hands of the midwife. Instant and unconditional love bloomed in him fast and hard. For her. His daughter. Perfect in every way.

Flora feathered her lips over her daughter's head. 'I've ached for you for ever,' she whispered.

'And I have ached for you both,' he breathed, unable to stop his confession.

Because he *had* ached for this all his life. Unconditional love. To receive it. To give it. To be a family.

With a smile and a nod, all the necessities of the miracle of birth complete, the midwife slipped out of the room unseen by either Raffaele or Flora, leaving the new parents with awe and wonderment brimming in their tear-glazed eyes to introduce themselves to their daughter.

'I'm so very thankful you chose me to love, Flora,' he said.

'We chose each other,' she corrected.

'It was fate.'

'Destiny,' she said huskily.

Their worlds had collided one fateful night in London and since then they had been bound together for ever. Not because of their baby, but because of love. And their baby was proof of that love. A love he could taste in the air.

He let it fill his lungs, feed his life's essence.

'I love you, Flora,' he said, wrapping his arms around his family.

She smoothed her fingers down their daughter's cheek. 'I love you too, Raffaele.'

Raffaele held his family to his chest—to his heart. Skin to skin. He embraced them with his love and vowed that he would never stop loving them...

* * * * *

If you couldn't get enough of
Bound by a Sicilian Secret,
then don't miss Lela May Wight's
debut for Harlequin Presents,
His Desert Bride by Demand*!*

Available now!